The Threat

Even the book morphs!
Flip the pages
and check it out!

Look for other ANIMORPHS® titles by K.A. Applegate:

#1 The Invasion
#2 The Visitor
#3 The Encounter
#4 The Message
#5 The Predator
#6 The Capture
#7 The Stranger
#8 The Alien
#9 The Secret
#10 The Android
#11 The Forgotten
#12 The Reaction
#13 The Change
#14 The Unknown
#15 The Escape
#16 The Warning
#17 The Underground
#18 The Decision
#19 The Departure
#20 The Discovery

<MEGAMORPHS>

#1 The Andalite's Gift
#2 In the Time of Dinosaurs

ANIMORPHS®

The Threat

K.A. Applegate

SCHOLASTIC INC.
New York Toronto London Auckland Sydney

Cover illustration by David B. Mattingly

ISBN 0-590-76254-0

12 11 10 9 8 7 6 5 4 3 2 1 8 9/9 0 1 2 3/0

Printed in the U.S.A. 40

First Scholastic printing, September 1998

For Miles and Coleman

Also for Michael and Jake

CHAPTER 1

My name is Jake.

And I was one sorry cockroach.

<Aaaaaahhhhh!> I yelled as I twirled and fell and spun downward toward the ground far below.

Not that I could see the ground. Cockroach eyes are strictly for close-up work. And they're not even good at that.

So I couldn't see the ground thousands of feet below. Nor could I see Marco, Cassie, Ax, and David, also cockroaches and also falling through the air.

I could hear them, though.

<Aaaaaahhhhh!> Marco yelled.

<Aaaaaahhhhh!> Cassie agreed.

Only Ax was silent. He's an Andalite. They

don't scream quite as much as humans. It's not that they're braver, it's more that they're a telepathic species. So I guess they just didn't evolve to do a lot of screaming.

<We're gonna dieeee!> David yelled in thought-speak panic.

<I do not believe the impact will kill us,> Ax said. <I don't believe our mass is sufficient to cause death when we impact.>

<He's right!> Cassie cried. <You can't kill a cockroach by dropping it. Not even from this high.>

<Unless that's water below us,> Marco said. <In which case we could hit the water and get chomped by some big hungry fish.>

<Should we demorph?> Ax wondered.

<No time,> I said. <We'd get bigger, more mass, and then when we hit we'd —>

I stopped falling. In an instant something hit me. But it hit me going sideways. A gigantic talon closed around me.

<That is you guys, right?> Rachel's thought-speak voice asked calmly. <I mean I figure, cockroaches falling through the air, gotta be you guys.>

<Yeah, you seldom see cockroaches at a thousand feet up,> Tobias agreed.

Rachel and Tobias had not been aboard the spacecraft. The spacecraft that had kidnapped the president's helicopter. The one we'd fallen out of. In cockroach morph.

Maybe I should back up and explain.

It all began when we discovered that the blue box — the morphing cube — had been found by a kid named David.

Well, no, actually it all began much earlier. Months ago, when Marco, Cassie, Rachel, Tobias, and I happened to be walking home from the mall by way of an abandoned construction site.

Which is where we saw the damaged spacecraft landing. And where we met Elfangor, an Andalite prince. Elfangor was dying. His enemies, the Yeerks, were hot on his trail. He was out of time.

So he did something Andalites don't usually do: He trusted some non-Andalites. Namely, the five of us. He told us that Earth was being invaded by a race of parasites called Yeerks.

The Yeerks are slugs, really. Not very impressive-looking or scary. But they have the ability to enter a brain — almost any brain — and take control of it. Absolute, complete, total control.

They've done this to the entire race of Gedds from their own home world. They've done it to the Hork-Bajir. They've done it to the Taxxons.

They are trying to do it to Homo sapiens. Humans. You and me. All of us.

Already, Elfangor said, there were thousands, maybe tens of thousands of human-Controllers. That is to say, humans who had a Yeerk in their heads controlling their words and actions. The invasion was under way. The Andalite forces had been beaten in orbit around Earth. It might be a very long time before any more Andalite forces could come. Too long.

Basically, if someone was going to stop the Yeerks, it would have to be humans. Us. Five normal kids. Five average, everyday, mall-crawling, behind on their homework, not sure about their haircuts, awkward around members of the opposite sex, sometimes smart, sometimes dumb kids.

On the Yeerks' side they had faster-than-light spacecraft, thousands of impossible-to-detect human-Controllers, Dracon beam weapons, and seven-foot-tall, bladed Hork-Bajir warriors. On our side we had . . . we had nothing.

Except.

Except that Elfangor gave us something: the power to morph. The power to become any animal we could touch. He transformed us with the blue box. And since that awful night when Prince Elfangor died at the hands of the Yeerk leader, Visser Three, we have used those powers to fight them.

Sometimes we even win.

We found Elfangor's younger brother, Aximili. (We call him "Ax.") That made six of us. And that was it. Five kids and one Andalite against the might of the Yeerk Empire.

Just us six. Until . . .

Until David found the blue box. We assumed it had been destroyed. It hadn't.

Now, we had it hidden. But too late to stop the trouble that followed.

David found the box and bad things started happening. Bottom line: Both his parents were taken by the Yeerks. They were infested with Yeerks. They are both Controllers now.

What could we do? We had to use the blue box to make David one of us. The sixth Animorph.

But the timing could not have been worse. We were just starting on what would be our most vital mission.

The leaders of the United States, Japan, Russia, Germany, England, and France were meeting in secret to try and work out the problems in the Middle East.

We learned that one of those leaders was in fact a Controller. And we knew that all the rest were targeted by the Yeerks.

The Yeerks were going to try to use the conference to infest the leaders of the entire free world.

If we let that happen, that was the ball game. Earth was done for. We had to try and stop it.

On our way to scope out the Marriott resort where the meeting was supposed to happen, we saw a stealth-shielded Yeerk spacecraft kidnap the President's helicopter. Or maybe it wasn't the actual President's helicopter. It might have been a decoy.

Confused yet? Not as confused as we were.

The Yeerks stunned everyone on the chopper and then used holographic projections to make it look like the helicopter was still flying along. They dragged someone from the helicopter. Some-one with a gash in the bottom of his shoe.

Look, we were cockroaches at the time. The shoe was all we could see. We assumed the Yeerks would infest this guy. The president, or whoever it was.

But no. Visser Three merely acquired his DNA so he could morph him.

See, Visser Three is the only Yeerk in all the galaxy to have managed to take control of an An-dalite body. He's the only Yeerk who can morph.

Now he could morph Mr. Slashed Shoe. Who-ever *he* was.

Sigh.

Do you see why my grade point average has dropped? I have to deal with this kind of stuff. It's enough to make your head explode.

But at least we didn't splat or end up as fish food. Tobias and Rachel snagged us out of thin air and carried us to safety. Now all we had to do was deal with our possibly strange new Animorph, David, while finding a way to save the leaders of the free world. And not get killed.

<Something's bothering me,> Marco said as Tobias and Rachel set us safely down in a secluded area between sand dunes.

<What's bothering you?> I said.

<Well, I'm in a cockroach body, just fell out of the bottom of a spaceship belonging to brain-stealing alien slugs while trying to save the president of the United States, was rescued by a girl who's temporarily a bald eagle and a guy who's permanently a red-tailed hawk . . . and yet, it all seems normal somehow. Like, okay, that's just to be expected. It's finally happened, hasn't it?>

<What's finally happened?> I asked.

<I've gone insane,> Marco said. <Deedly deeedly deedly looopy! Nutso. Insane in the membrane.>

<Yeah, well, keep it together,> I said, trying to sound like the leader I supposedly am. <The entire human race depends on us winning this battle.>

<Poor human race,> Marco said.

It was a joke. Just not a very funny one.

CHAPTER 2

We demorphed in the dunes. Five of us had no problems. One of us had a serious problem.

"Rachel, Cassie. Look the other way," I said.

David was the new Animorph. He had not yet learned how to morph clothing. Actually, none of us could morph it very well. We could only morph skintight clothing that ended up being a kind of mishmash of bike shorts, leotards, and T-shirts.

Basically, in our morphing outfits we looked pathetic.

But not as pathetic as poor David.

<I'll take care of it,> Tobias said. He flapped away, catching the salt-heavy breeze off the water and soaring up and out of sight beyond the dunes.

Tobias was still a hawk. Tobias may always be a hawk. He spent more than two hours in the morph and was trapped in it. Now he has regained his morphing powers. But he cannot return to being permanently human without losing his ability to morph.

<I do not understand humans and their strange beliefs when it comes to clothing,> Ax said. He was in his own Andalite form. His four hooves sank deep in the sand. Tobias would let us know if anyone was coming close enough to see Ax.

<You wear artificial skin and artificial hooves. When it is cold that makes sense. But when it is warm it seems strange. And you get so concerned when some article of clothing is missing or worn in the wrong way.>

"You mean like that time you wore socks on your hands?" Marco asked him.

"Or the time you wore underwear on the outside of your pants?" Rachel added, still discreetly turned away.

"You know, maybe this is funny to you guys," David said. "But it's not all that funny to me. What if someone came along?"

I laughed. "Well, David, if they did, I think they'd probably notice the four-eyed, scorpion-tailed, blue, half-deer-looking alien before they worried about you."

Just then Tobias swept in on the breeze, turned, dropped toward us, and let loose of a pair of swim trunks. Orange. And a T-shirt bearing a Grateful Dead logo. Both had price tags still attached.

David snagged them before they hit the ground.

<Remind me we have to return those to the Kahuna Beach Shop,> Tobias said.

"You stole them?" Cassie asked.

<No, I *borrowed* them. Besides, I'm a bird. Birds are not capable of stealing. What are they going to do, arrest me?>

"We'll find a way to get the money to the store," I said. "We don't want to even start down that path. In an emergency like this, maybe we can grab something. But we have to make it right later. That's the rule."

David dressed quickly and Cassie and Rachel were allowed to turn around.

"About time," Rachel muttered. "I've been staring at a dead sand crab."

"You know, it *would* be amazing," David said.

"What would be?" I asked.

He shrugged. "Us, with our powers? We could take anything we wanted. We could like morph into cheetahs or whatever, run into some jewelry store, grab the diamonds, and get away at sixty miles an hour. What could anyone do? We'd be outta there. Plus, we'd morph back to humans."

"Let's do that," Marco said dryly. "Right after we figure out how to keep the Yeerks from turning the most powerful leaders in the world into alien-infested zombies. As soon as we're done with that, we start ripping off jewelry stores."

"Hey, I was just kidding," David said. "I guess I forgot you're the only one allowed to make jokes, Marco."

I glanced at Marco. Was he mad at the shot? Yes, a little. I looked at David. He *had* been kidding, right?

Later I'd have to talk to Cassie about it. Cassie was a lot better at knowing what people were thinking and feeling than I was. She'd know. Hopefully.

In the meantime, I had to remember to treat David like any other member of the group. It wasn't so bad that David and Marco didn't totally get along. There were times when we all got on one another's nerves. It was natural.

"Okay, time to get serious here," I said. "They caught us by surprise. Maybe they know that was us scurrying around up there, maybe they don't. But one way or the other, we have to get inside that resort and get busy."

"We have to get past the greatest security in

the world just to get into that place," Rachel said. "We have to go by air. But we can't use bird-of-prey morphs. That'd be slightly noticeable."

"No problem," Cassie said. "It's the beach. There's one kind of bird no one can keep off the beach. Seagulls."

"Yeah, well, I don't have a seagull morph," David pointed out. "But I'll bet I could morph back into golden eagle morph and bring one down."

I winced a little at his eagerness. The basic idea was sound. Only there was no need to have David morph again. "Tobias?" I yelled up to him. He was riding the breeze, almost stationary above us. He spilled air and dropped down closer. "Sorry to keep sending you out for things, but can you get a seagull?"

"Alive?" Cassie added.

<Can I grab a gull? Puh-leeze. Can Michael Jordan hit a three-pointer? They're just rats with wings.>

"Tobias is like really into the whole bird thing, isn't he?" David commented.

"Tobias just has some fairly definite opinions about birds," I said. "He respects most eagles, owls, and other hawks. Looks down on gulls and pigeons. And he absolutely hates jays, crows, and golden eagles."

David laughed. "He's like a racist or something, only with birds instead of people."

"All those birds are different species," Cassie pointed out. "Humans are all one species. Not really a very good comparison."

David shrugged, and looked a little sullen. "Whatever."

I started to say something, then stopped myself. I was feeling edgy and strange. We were about to try to violate a resort with security that would make Fort Knox look like a Wal-Mart during a clearance sale. We were up against security from France, Britain, Japan, Germany, Russia, and the United States. Plus, we were competing against the Yeerks, who had already infiltrated the place to some extent.

And I was going in with no plan, no clue, and a new guy I wasn't totally used to yet. How would this guy do in a battle? How would he do when it got really rough? He'd done okay when we were roaches being chased around. He hadn't panicked. But things could get worse. They could get way worse.

I noticed Cassie looking at me, reading the worry on my face. I looked up at the sky like I was searching for Tobias. When I lowered my face again I had on my "fearless leader" expression. No point in making everyone else nervous, too.

Tobias actually did appear just then, carrying

a squirming, kicking, flapping, very, very annoyed seagull in his talons.

<That was actually fun,> Tobias said with a laugh. <Snatched him out of midair while he was diving on some guy's sandwich. And, as much as I *so* did not want to, I acquired the gull. David's not the only one without a gull morph.>

Cassie took the poor gull from Tobias and comforted it. Cassie handles lots of animals. She brought it to David.

"I'm starting to get this down," David said, pressing one hand against the gull's wing. "Just focus and his DNA is mine."

"Yeah," I agreed. "Easy after a while. So let's do it. We morph to gulls, we skim on down the beach, and land in the resort. See what we see."

"One big point," Cassie said. "Act like gulls, okay? The humans won't be looking for trouble from seagulls. But the Yeerks will."

CHAPTER 3

<“Off we go, into the wild blue yonder, flying high into the sun!”> Marco sang.

<Marco, why are you singing?> Rachel asked.

<It’s some old movie on the Movie Channel about Air Force pilots. That was their song. “Off we go, into the wild blue yonder, flying high into the sun.”>

<Marco? *Why* are you *still* singing when clearly I want you to shut up?>

<“Off we go, into the . . .” Hey! Whoa! Pizza Hut! The guy down there on the blue beach towel. He’s got an entire large pizza!>

<Is he going to eat all that himself?> David asked eagerly. <No way one guy eats a large pizza.>

Many morphs have powerful instincts you have to learn to deal with. Like the soulless, automaton obedience of ants or the raging, insane hunger of a shrew. You deal with it. In the case of seagull morphs, the instincts were not exactly dangerous to us, but they were very hard to shake off.

Basically, seagulls are scavengers. Which means they have an amazing talent for spotting anything that looks even slightly like available food. We were above the sand, skimming and dodging out along the surf line like typical gulls. Ahead of us, up the beach, was the line of trees and the tan stucco wall that marked the edge of the resort.

We were not the only gulls around. Not by a long shot. In fact, about seventeen gulls had also spotted the pizza. They were wheeling and hovering and going "Squeeet! Squeeet! Squeeet!" and "Aw! Aw! Aw!"

The guy with the pizza was looking nervous.

<Keep flying,> I said, although I, too, had to fight the weird desire to dive on some pepperoni. I mean, seriously, a large pan pizza for one guy? No reason why he couldn't toss a couple slices off to one side so we . . .

But pizza was not the point.

<Fries!> Rachel cried.

<Okay, now look,> I said, <we are about to try and —>

<Oh! Oh! Fried chicken!> Marco said. <Hey, Tobias. If a seagull eats chicken, is that like cannibalism or something?>

<That depends. Extra crispy or regular?>

At last we were nearing the stucco wall. Seagull eyes aren't as penetrating as bird-of-prey eyes, but they are still very good. I spotted a dark-suited man standing in the shadow of the row of tall trees. He wore dark sunglasses. He was talking into a handheld radio. He was staring in our direction, gazing out over the beach with a very serious amount of concentration.

<Gee, could that guy look any more like Secret Service?> Rachel said with a laugh. <And there's another one just ten feet away, along the wall.>

<Of course *they're* Secret Service,> David said. <But so are some of the people lying out here on the beach. With something like this, probably half the people on the beach are security.>

<And of course you're the big expert because your dad is a spy,> Marco said with a definite sneer.

<He's with the National Security Agency, that's right,> David said.

<Yeah? Well now he's with the Yeerk Security Agency,> Marco muttered.

<Shut up, Marco!> I snapped. <That was over the line.>

Marco pouted for a moment or two as we oh-so-casually closed the distance between us and the wall. <You're right. I was out of line. Sorry.>

David didn't say anything. I couldn't blame him. Usually Marco knows how far to take things. Maybe I was wrong to think Marco's attitude toward David was totally normal. Maybe we had a problem there.

We didn't fly over the wall all together in some kind of formation. We did it one at a time, crossing in various locations. The security guys seemed indifferent. No big surprise. There were gulls all over the place. In fact, looking around, it was impossible to know which of the white birds was one of us and which was just a plain old seagull.

<This is easy,> David said. <What's the big deal?>

<As long as we just want to fly around, no big deal,> I agreed. <But we need to get inside some of these buildings. Maybe *all* these buildings.>

<The question is, where do we begin? And how?> Ax said.

The resort had a dozen or more buildings. The main building was a large, multistory, modern hotel shaped like an "L." There was a lower, two-story portion stuck off to one side. Probably a ballroom or whatever.

Nestled in the crook of the "L" shape was a pool with a bar and a changing area. And down by the water were cabins, like individual homes separated from the others by hedges and trees.

The grounds were lush with trimmed grass and precise shrubbery and trees. A nine-hole golf course began at the back side of the main hotel. From the air we could easily see the two presidential helicopters resting on a grass landing area. Uniformed Marine guards stood at attention by the doors of the helicopters.

<Okay, there is definitely some security on this place,> Marco said. <Guys on the roof, guys in the bushes, guys sitting in cars, guys out on the golf course pretending to play golf. It looks like *Men in Black 2* around here. These guys all have the same suit.>

Then I spotted something that raised my spirits a little. <Look! Canine teams!>

Below me a German shepherd walked with yet another "Man in Black." The dog was sniffing in bushes. Either looking for a place to pee or searching for bombs.

<Maybe we could morph German shepherds and get in as part of the canine team,> I said, realizing as I said it that it probably wouldn't work.

A truck was delivering food to the loading dock at the back of the hotel. No less than four guys in dark suits were checking the crates as they came off the truck.

The Men in Black had earpieces, like people being interviewed on TV. And they seemed to talk to their wrists a lot. There were microphones barely visible just up in their sleeves.

<Here's an idea. Let's give up,> Marco said. <This would be totally depressing even if we didn't have to worry about some of these guys being Controllers.>

I was starting to agree. <Every square inch of this entire place is being watched,> I said. <We can't morph or demorph anywhere around it. We need to get inside to learn what we want to learn, but that would mean going insect basically. And the problem with any insect morph is that we'd have to morph the bug way outside the compound, which leaves us traveling a long, long way as spiders or cockroaches or flies. None of which can see well enough to travel those distances without getting lost.>

<Or eaten,> Rachel added darkly.

<You guys could morph fleas and get onto someone who we knew was going inside the compound,> Tobias suggested.

<But fleas are useless for seeing, and they aren't much good at hearing,> Cassie said. <We'd

get in, but once inside we'd get nothing. And how would we ever get back out again?>

<Are we beat?> Marco asked, incredulous.

I sighed. <Maybe. Only we can't be. No matter what the risk, we have to get inside and — AAAAHHHH!>

The pain came out of nowhere. Suddenly, for no reason, I'd felt a wave of agony that seemed to sizzle and fry every cell in my body.

<Jake, what's happening?> Cassie cried.

<AAAAAHHHH!> Ax screamed.

<What's going on?> David asked nervously.

The pain was gone, but my brain was still burning from the memory. I looked down, around, everywhere. What? What had caused . . . ?

There below me and ahead, not fifty feet away, stood a security man, like all the others. He had a bald patch on his head, something you notice when you're a bird. He wore dark glasses, like all the others.

But unlike all the others, he was watching the birds.

CHAPTER 4

<AAAAAHHHHH!> It was Tobias's turn.

I stared at the bald man. I saw where he was looking. He was looking at a gull that had suddenly jerked in mid-flight.

Tobias?

<It's that guy!> I said, suddenly certain. <That bald guy! He's doing it!>

I watched the bald man casually shift his gaze to another seagull. This seagull, too, spasmed in midair. It recovered and began to haul wing out of there.

Not one of us. A regular gull.

<Ax! What is that guy doing? I don't see any weapon.>

Ax sounded as shaken as I was. <He may . . . he may be using a very low-power Dracon beam. Possibly hidden on his body, with the sunglasses used as emitters.>

<Are you telling me he can shoot whatever he's looking at?> I said.

<Yes. It will cause intense pain. As you may have noticed.>

That was as close as Ax ever got to making a joke. And having been on the receiving end of the bald guy's "look," I really didn't find it all that humorous.

<So he's a Controller chasing away the birds,> Tobias said. <He doesn't kill us because that would be too obvious — dead birds dropping everywhere.>

<Chasing away possible Andalites in morph,> Marco agreed.

The Yeerks still think we're a small band of Andalites. They have no clue we're humans with Andalite morphing powers.

<Oh, man!> Cassie moaned. <He's looking at — AAAAAHHHH!>

<Cassie!>

<Oh. Oh, that hurt. Oh man, I'm not kidding here. That was like a full-body dental visit without Novocain.>

<Cassie. Bail. Fly away. That's what a gull

would do. But not everyone at once!> I added quickly. <We can't move like we know what's happening.>

<We have to stay here and let that guy zap us?> David demanded. <We should either run or go kick his butt for him!>

I had felt the pain. I knew how awful it was. But I couldn't let everyone turn tail and run. Not all at once. We had to be normal gulls. Still, I knew how the others felt. I felt it, too, floating helpless and exposed in midair, waiting for the bald man to hit me again.

<He's looking at me!> David yelled. <What am I supposed to do?>

<Nothing,> I grated. <Take it. Then you can bail.>

<AAAAAHHHHH!>

I felt like the creep of the universe making David take the hit. But we couldn't give ourselves away. That would confirm to the Yeerks that we were attempting to enter the facility.

I saw David spasm. I knew the pain he had just endured. The part of my brain that wasn't busy feeling guilty wondered how he'd react.

<Okay, *that* was a major ouchie!> David said. <*Now* can I get out of here?>

<Yeah, fly,> I said. <And by the way, David? Good job.>

<Thanks,> he said, sounding sincere. Then in a sarcastic tone he added, <Thanks a lot.>

I watched him fly away. Ax and Tobias and Rachel had all managed to casually, naturally circle away out of the bald man's line of sight. But I was still there.

The bald man looked at me.

I would have gritted my teeth if I'd had teeth. The pain hit me as bad as the first time, and I cried out just the same.

Then I flew away, following the others and feeling that maybe the free world really was doomed this time around. Because as far as I could see, we were beat before we even got started.

CHAPTER 5

We left. We went home. At least, Marco, Rachel, Cassie, and I went home. Ax's home is a few billion miles away. Tobias's home is his favorite tree overlooking the meadow that is his territory.

As for David, he didn't have a home. No home, no family. None that he could contact, anyway. He couldn't even be seen in his own body. The Yeerks knew him and they were looking for him.

So he went home with Cassie, back to the barn that is the Wildlife Rehabilitation Clinic. She had made a place for him in the hayloft.

Obviously, that wasn't going to last. Another problem for me to try to figure out. Along with saving the leaders of the free world. David would just have to tough it out.

How quickly would the Yeerks move? The President was already at the resort. The other world leaders were arriving over the next few hours. Would the Yeerks wait till they were all assembled? Or would they try to pick them off one by one?

I felt this huge hurry poking at me. Every minute lost was a possible disaster. But our first attempt had been a total loss. And we weren't ready for another run.

I got home to find my parents both sitting in the living room, kind of staring into space. My first thought was, *Uh-oh, I did something wrong.*

But as soon as they saw me they both got up and hugged me. So right away I knew this was something truly bad.

"Thank goodness you're home," my mother said.

"We were worried," my dad said.

"Why? I was just out with Marco."

"Something has happened," my dad said solemnly. "Maybe you should sit down."

"Is it Tom?" I demanded.

"Is what Tom?" Tom asked. He came in right behind me, giving me the creepy feeling that he'd been following me.

"Tom, you need to hear this, too," my mother said. "Both of you sit down."

"Who died?" Tom said, joking. Or to be more accurate, the Yeerk in his head made the dumb joke because it was just the kind of dumb joke Tom would make.

My mom and dad gave Tom this hollow-eyed look.

My mother said, "It's your cousin, Saddler. He was riding his bike and was hit by a car. He's alive, but the injuries are very severe. He's in intensive care."

I'm ashamed to admit that my first reaction was not "poor Saddler." Instead, I wondered what impact this would have on my plans. Partly that's because Saddler was not a cousin I was close to. He's two years older, and to be honest, kind of a jerk. When we were little and our parents made us play together, he was the kind of kid who'd break something and then blame me.

It was pretty awful to think he was so badly hurt. But at the same time, I was trying to figure out how this affected me. Saddler and his family lived in a small town about a hundred miles away.

"Your mom and I are going to drive down right away to help Ellen and George with the other kids. They think they'll probably move Saddler to Children's Hospital here in town in a day or two, if . . . I mean . . ."

My mom cut in. "This means you two will be on your own today and tomorrow."

Tom and I exchanged a look. Both of us were calculating what this meant. We each had a hidden agenda. Tom didn't know mine. If Tom ever found out what I did when I wasn't at home or at school, that would be the end of my freedom. Probably the end of my life.

"Then, after Saddler is moved here, his parents and the kids will probably stay with us for at least a few days."

That pretty well froze the blood in my veins. Saddler has three siblings: Justin, Brooke, and Forrest. Forrest is two years old and is, basically, the devil. I'm exaggerating, but only slightly.

"Why can't they stay with Rachel's family?" Tom asked. "They're cousins, too."

"Well, since Rachel's mom and dad got divorced, Ellen and George haven't felt like they were all that close to Rachel's mom."

"Lucky Rachel," Tom muttered.

This all left me feeling even more disturbed than before. I felt guilty for not feeling sorry for Saddler right away. I felt guilty for caring that his family would be staying with us. I even felt guilty for thinking it was a relief that my mom and dad would be gone for the next day or so.

All that, piled on top of the fact that I felt guilty because while I was sitting around feeling

guilty the leaders of the free world were possibly being infested with Yeerks.

I felt like my head was going to burst. I felt like I needed to sleep for about fourteen hours.

But I wasn't going to sleep. Not that night. Or the next. In fact, it was going to be a long time before I slept again.

CHAPTER 6

My parents drove off, but I didn't exactly declare a national holiday and throw a party. No time.

Instead I spent the evening doing the research I should have done earlier. I sat at my computer, plugged in to the Web, and read everything I could find about the conference, the leaders who would be there, the Marriott resort itself, the security services of each nation, everything.

Then I saw it: an article about the new prime minister of France. The one whose wife always, always, *always* traveled with her two Chihuahuas. Now, *that* could be useful.

"Ah-hah!"

"Ah-hah, what?"

I spun in my chair. It was Tom, sticking his head into my room. On my computer monitor was the article about the French chief.

Don't act guilty! I silently ordered myself. But I clicked the window closed anyway.

"Are you gonna tie up that line all night?" Tom demanded. "Someone might want to make a phone call. It's ten o'clock, anyway. Your bed-tiiiiime," he said, drawing out the last word.

"Shut up," I said. "Just because Mom and Dad aren't here, that doesn't make you —"

"Oh, yes it does. I am the All-Powerful Tom," he said.

Once again, I had this weird urge to say, "You know what, Tom? I know all about you. I know what you are. So how about if we just cut to the chase?"

What I really said was, "I'm done, anyway." I moved the mouse to "Sign off" and clicked once.

"Don't forget to brush your teeth," Tom said mockingly.

He closed the door. Had he seen what was on my screen? Probably not. Even if he had, so what? So I was interested in the French government.

Yeah. That made sense. What with my lifelong interest in European heads of state.

I sighed. Then . . .

Deedly-deeedly-deedly.

The phone rang. I hesitated. It was late for anyone to call. Probably Mom or Dad checking in.

I picked it up.

"Did you get that?" Tom yelled from down the hall.

"Yeah!" I yelled back. Then, in a normal voice, "Hello?"

"Hi, Jake, it's Cassie."

I felt a little tingle on the back of my neck. Cassie sounded cheerful. But that was because we never trusted the phones to be safe.

"Hi, Cassie, what's up?"

"Hey, you know what? I heard *Letterman* got canceled. Is that true? No more Dave?"

Now it was more than a tingle. Of course Letterman wasn't canceled. Cassie had just been looking for a way to say "Dave." As in David.

David was missing.

"Did you check *TV Guide*?"

"No. I looked everywhere else, though. Everywhere."

"Well, don't worry about it. He'll be there at the usual place, the usual time."

We hung up. We both knew. David was missing and I was on my way, as soon as I could get away safely. I'd be "at the usual place."

Twenty minutes later Tom came to check on

me. I was in my bed. Asleep. Or at least I looked asleep. I lay there in the dark, listening. Then I heard the faint sound of the front door opening and closing.

Tom was leaving. Yeerk business, no doubt.

"Yeerks make lousy baby-sitters," I muttered under my breath.

I morphed to brown bat and flew out of my open window. Bats aren't the fastest flyers in the world, but it was a moonless night, and I didn't want to risk running into power lines or anything that would be invisible.

I found Cassie and Rachel at the barn. It was a bit creepy at night. The lights were kept very low. Just enough to make out the rows of wire cages and to see vague shapes pacing or standing or snoring within.

Cassie looked worried. Rachel, as always, looked great. I demorphed and stood there, barefoot and shivering in bike shorts and T-shirt.

"Hey, Rachel. You must have morphed to get here so fast," I said. "So how come you have regular clothes on?"

Cassie rolled her eyes. "Didn't you know? Rachel keeps a couple of outfits here at the barn."

"Is it a crime to want to look good?" Rachel asked self-mockingly.

"Good grief," I said. "So what's the deal?"

"The deal is, David went to sleep up in the loft around nine. Early. Said he was tired. I checked on him. At ten I remembered that I forgot to give that deer with the bullet wound her meds, so I came back out. No David."

CHAPTER 7

"Did you try and reach Marco?"

Cassie nodded. "He can't come. His dad's out on a date, and when he comes back he's sure to check on Marco."

"I guess the question is: How did David leave here? On foot or on the wing?"

"The other question is why?" Rachel pointed out. "And where did he go? And while we're at it, doesn't he realize he's destroying my sleep with this stupid game?"

"Okay, look, you two have your owl morphs. One of you go and look for Ax and Tobias. They can help. I'll go to wolf morph, see if he left a scent trail. No, wait. What if someone sees me? Better do Homer."

Homer is my dog.

"I'll go for Tobias," Rachel said. "And Ax."

I was already morphing. Already feeling the long, shaggy fur sprouting from my hands and arms and chest.

"Um, Jake? You can't morph to dog in here. You know how dogs get around animals," Cassie warned.

"Oh. Yeah." I smiled with what was left of my human mouth. I had morphed Homer several times before. And it wasn't that his dog instincts were so overpowering or anything. It's just that he had a secret weapon for undermining my self-control: He was happy. As in HAPPY! And a dog surrounded by scared rodents and skunks and raccoons was just about as HAPPY as a living creature could be.

It's hard to resist happiness. It tends to kind of carry you away.

I opened the big, creaking barn door and went back outside. Hobbled, because my legs were bending and shrinking and my feet were already more like paws. Cassie followed.

Still no moon out. Clouds obscured the stars. It was as black as night gets. The only light came from the faint, distant porch lights from the nearest subdivision. And a light someone had left on in Cassie's house.

I finished morphing Homer. I felt my face

bulge out and out. I felt the teeth multiply and grow in my mouth. I felt my ears crawling up the side of my head.

My legs bent and shrank till I fell forward onto pads that had replaced my palms. My tail wagged. And I felt that amazing rush of giddy, idiot, dog happiness.

What had I been so worried about? It was nighttime, I was free, I could clearly hear some small animal scurrying over behind the bushes, I wasn't especially hungry. Life was great!

I looked expectantly at Cassie. Did she want to play? I crouched low in front, making the signal of an invitation to dog play.

Fortunately, Cassie had enough sense to decline.

"No, thank you," she said. "I don't think we're here to play."

We weren't?

Oh, right. We weren't.

But, hey! What was that smell? Was that . . . yes! It was dog poop! Not my poop. But definitely dog poop!

Where? I sniffed. Okay, over there. I trotted toward the source of the smell. Hmmm. Not fresh. This was old dog poop. At least a couple of days old.

That didn't mean it was totally useless. But fresh dog poop was really far more interesting.

Stale dog poop was only slightly more interesting than cat poop. And let's face it: No one cares about cat poop.

"I think we kind of have to focus, Jake," Cassie said as firmly as she could.

<What? Oh, yeah. I was just . . . you know, investigating.>

"Uh-huh."

"We need your nose, but not for that."

<Yeah, okay. Back to business.> I focused on the job at hand. Or I tried, at least. I mean, I sounded serious for Cassie's sake, but come on, what was there to be all grim about?

Life was a party!

"By the way, I meant to tell you I have an idea for how we can break into the resort. It's a morph that—"

<Wait a minute. Is this idea going to make me feel better or just creep me out?> I interrupted.

Cassie laughed. "Maybe we should talk about it later. Here." She handed me a T-shirt. "It's the shirt David wore yesterday."

I sniffed it once. No more was needed. Because I knew right away that David had in fact walked away from the barn. His trail might as well have been marked with orange traffic cones.

This wasn't as fun as chasing a stick. But it was some kind of game, at least. And I liked Cassie.

If only she had a stick.

CHAPTER 8

I followed David's scent as Cassie floated in absolute silence overhead. Her owl's wings made no sound. Not even to my ears.

<He stopped here,> I said. We were a thousand yards from the barn in the middle of a field. <He morphed. I'm getting a new scent.>

I sniffed carefully at the ground, going around in a circle. <The idiot!> I yelled, suddenly too angry to be dog HAPPY. <He went into that lion morph you hooked him up with.>

<Maybe he just wanted to try it out,> Cassie said. <We all used to do things like that.>

<Yeah,> I agreed. <But a lion? This close to people's homes?>

<I seem to remember you morphing to tiger and running around on people's roofs, Jake.>

<Oh. Yeah.>

I followed the lion scent. We headed across the fields of Cassie's farm and plunged into woods. Cassie kept pace effortlessly. And after a while a second silent owl and a much noisier hawk caught up to us.

<I couldn't find Ax,> Rachel said. <But Tobias is here.>

<Yeah, lucky me,> Tobias grumbled.

We emerged again from the woods, and now we were close to a major road. On the far side it was a built-up strip: Taco Bell, Mickey D's, a tire place, a couple of gas stations, and a Holiday Inn.

I sniffed the ground again. <He demorphed here.> I trotted forward closer to the road, closer to the cars blazing past at sixty miles an hour. <Here he morphed again. The golden eagle.>

I took a deep breath. I had a bad feeling about this. I began to demorph. I wanted to be able to look around as a human to see what David had seen.

Human once more, and not at all HAPPY, I looked up and down the street. "So. Maybe he just came to snag some food. Maybe he was hungry."

<I left him some chips up in the loft,> Cassie said.

"Maybe he had a craving for a Big Mac. Cassie, did he say anything to you tonight?"

<He was complaining about missing his old room. His pet snake. His stuff. TV.>

I nodded. "Yep. TV." I pointed at the Holiday Inn. "Cassie, Tobias, Rachel? Go take a look. I'll be right there."

Ten minutes later, I was in the carpeted hall of the Holiday Inn. I knocked at the door number "2135." I could hear the television inside. Then the TV went silent.

"David, it's me, Jake. I know you're in there."

The door opened. David was wearing sweat-pants and a T-shirt. It was stuff I'd loaned him. Obviously, he'd taught himself to morph clothing like the rest of us.

I didn't wait to be invited. I stepped inside. The TV was still on, but muted.

"What, exactly, are you doing here?" I demanded, not very calmly.

David shrugged. "Hanging out. Watching some tube. Sleeping in a normal bed. What's that, a crime?"

"Yeah, it is a crime," I said. "You didn't pay for this room."

"It was empty. So what?"

I pointed at the broken window we'd spotted from outside. "You broke a window to get in."

David smirked. "Hey, a bird broke a window, okay? A bird used a rock to dive-bomb the glass. Is that a crime? I don't think so. Officer, arrest that eagle? That's not happening."

"You're not talking to someone who doesn't know what's what, okay? The eagle morph is just a body and basic instincts. The mind is yours. Eagles don't bust into Holiday Inns. That was you."

David flopped back onto the bed and picked up the remote control. He started flipping channels, ignoring me.

"Listen, David, we don't break laws. Not unless absolutely necessary. We don't hurt innocent people. We have to control how we behave. We're not a bunch of criminals. Like on the beach when we needed clothing? I already mailed the money to the shop. Are you going to do that here?"

David stopped channel surfing. "How's it end for me, Jake?" he asked. "I have no home, all right? My family wants to turn me over to the Yeerks. What am I supposed to do? Keep living in that barn? It's easy for you, Jake. You have a family. You have a home. You all have homes. You all sleep in beds at night and watch TV and eat at a table."

"Not all of us," I said. "Not Tobias. Not Ax."

"Ax isn't even human. Neither is Tobias. I *am*. I'm human, like you and Marco and Cassie and Rachel, and all of you have homes. All of you can walk around the mall without having every Controller around come down on you."

"It's a bad situation," I said. "It stinks."

"Yeah. And what are you going to do about it, Jake?"

"I . . . look, we can only handle so many things at once, okay? Right now the leaders of the most powerful nations on Earth are being targeted by the Yeerks. I *feel* the clock ticking. I know your life sucks, okay? But I can't figure that out right now. Later. After this mission is over."

David gave me a look that was pure cynicism. "Yeah. Right. Well, how about this, Jake? I'll handle my life. You be the big boss of the Animorphs, and I'll take care of me."

An answer to David's challenge had formed in my mind. The words were right there. But they were harsh. And if I spoke them, I'd cross a line with David. A line I might not be able to uncross.

"It's like school and home, okay?" David continued. "It's like being an Animorph is school, and you're the teacher or the principal or whatever. But then, after I go home, you don't tell me what to do anymore."

I shook my head. "No, that's not what it's

like, David. I don't want to come down on you, but the way it is is like this: You want to go around using your powers in selfish ways, then we can't have you around. You're just a danger to us. And you're against what we stand for."

His eyes widened. He rolled off the bed and stood up. "Are you threatening me?"

"No. Just telling you the way it is. We're the only family you have now, David. The only people you can trust. The only people who can help you. We're all you have. Deal with it."

He shot me a sullen, resentful look. I couldn't blame him. I sounded like someone's father saying, "As long as you live in my house, you'll follow my rules." I sounded like I was threatening him.

I was.

"Let's go," I said.

We went.

CHAPTER 9

Cassie had said she had an idea for getting past the security at the resort. She'd also admitted it would creep me out.

And, as always, she was honest.

It was the next day. We actually had to skip school. Marco, Rachel, Cassie, and me. It was something we'd never done all together before. It was risky. We couldn't have people noticing the fact that we were out of school together.

But the situation was desperate.

We were not in the barn. Cassie's father would be working there during the day. We were in the woods near Tobias's meadow.

"See, the problem is, anything bigger than a bug is going to be noticed by the Controllers who are in the security teams," Cassie explained. "But all the insect morphs we have are wrong for this job. Too much distance to cover for a cockroach. Same thing with a fly or an ant. Too much distance with senses that are not much good at dealing with faraway objects."

"Uh-huh," Marco said, nodding grimly. "And so what have you come up with, I hesitate to ask?"

She removed a glass jar from her backpack and held it out for us to see. Inside it was a large, brilliant green insect with two sets of wings.

"What is that, a dragonfly?" David asked.

"Yeah. Dragonfly," Cassie confirmed. "Look closely and you'll notice the eyes. They are huge, relative to the size of the body. They completely cover the dragonfly's head."

"No way," David said.

Cassie ignored him. "The housefly morphs we have feed on garbage, carrion, so on. So their sense of sight doesn't have to be great. But dragonflies eat other flying insects. They snag mosquitoes right out of the air. And since we know they don't have echolocation like bats have, they must be using the sense of sight to hunt."

"Wait a minute," David said. "When we became cockroaches we almost got stomped!"

"Seven dragonflies all flying in there together?" Marco said skeptically. "What happens

if the Controllers realize there's this sudden plague of dragonflies?"

Cassie winced. "Well, I thought of that. So, see, only one person would morph the dragonfly. That person would get inside, find a place for the rest of us to demorph, and then morph something else to go spying around."

<I'm not understanding this,> Ax said. <How will the rest of us get inside with this single dragonfly?>

"Well . . ." Cassie said. "That's the part that is either beautiful or gross, depending on your point of view."

"Oh, I *so* don't want to hear this," Marco moaned.

"See, the dragonfly is so big, and such a powerful flyer, he can carry passengers."

We all considered that for a moment. All of us staring at Cassie.

<What kind of passengers, Cassie?> Tobias asked.

"Well . . . I think you could get six fleas lined up on —"

"Okay, okay, *that's* not happening," David said.

"One of us morphs a dragonfly, the rest of us morph fleas and climb on board like we're flying Delta?" Rachel demanded. "How would we even hold on? It'll be like being on a jet. On the *outside* of a jet!"

Cassie grinned. "Oh, the holding on part is easy. Fleas are excellent grippers. Besides, for extra safety, you just have to bite the dragonfly and not let go."

Once again we all stared at Cassie.

"You're a very disturbing person sometimes, Cassie," Marco said.

Rachel sighed. "Who's the lucky dragonfly who gets to have six fleas attached to him or her?"

"We can draw straws," I said.

"Wait a minute, we're *doing* this?" David cried. "Are you nuts?"

Marco pointed at David and said, "For once, I'm with him."

I bent over and plucked a handful of pine needles from the ground. I counted seven and broke one short. "Short needle morphs the dragonfly."

CHAPTER 10

I drew the short straw. So I was the one to stick my fingers into the jar and touch the dragonfly.

He seemed to be built of three elements: helicopter wings, gigantic eyes, and a ridiculously long blue-green tail. Actually the abdomen, but it looked like a stiff tail.

Cassie had also brought a flea for those who'd never morphed a flea. The plan was for me to morph the dragonfly, the others except for Tobias to morph the flea, and then Tobias would fly us all close to the resort and release us.

Easier said than done.

"This can't even be possible," David said. "I

mean, a flea? Look how big we are! The flea is like . . . like a grain of sand."

<It is possible,> Ax said. <The extra mass is extruded into Zero-space. Our own minds and brains are pushed into Zero-space and maintain contact with the morph by means of a —>

"What is he talking about?" David asked.

Rachel shrugged. "We don't have any idea. But he's right: It works. So just relax with it."

"I'm going to become a flea and I should just relax. A flea!"

He looked from one of us to the next, I guess waiting to see if it was all some big joke.

"I'm ready," I said. I took a deep breath and began the morph.

Every morph is different. And no morph ever makes logical sense. It's not like everything changes at once. It's not like if you're morphing a tiny insect you're going to start off with tiny insect legs. That would be gross enough. The reality is so much grosser.

See, in reality you might morph an ant and suddenly have these gigantic ant legs that then begin to shrink. Or you might be morphing an elephant and start off with this three-inch-long trunk.

So not only is morphing weird and illogical. It can be weird in different ways for different

people. And it can be weirder one time than the next.

I have morphed many, many times. If I morph another ten thousand times, I will still never, never get used to it.

I focused on the dragonfly with a fair amount of fear. I closed my eyes and began to change. Then, quite suddenly, my eyes were open again.

Only I hadn't opened them. I just didn't happen to have eyelids anymore. And my eyes . . .

"Oh. Oh, no," Cassie said in disgust. "Oh. Oh, guh."

"Man, I didn't need to see that," Rachel agreed.

"Okay, now *that* is gross," Marco said. "That is seriously gross."

The first things that had morphed were my eyes. I was standing there, big as my normal self, normal everywhere. Except for the fact that my entire head — everything but my mouth — was covered with two monstrous, bulging, iridescent insect eyeballs.

"Aaaahhh!" I commented calmly.

"That does it, I'm outta here!" David yelped. But he didn't move.

The world I saw was a blaze of eerie colors. Normal colors seemed to bleed with strange purples and intense reds. I couldn't see objects at all clearly, no forms, no edges.

"I can't see except a blur!" I yelled.

"You still have a human brain," Cassie said. "You need the dragonfly's visual cortex to interpret the dragonfly's eyes."

I could sense that I was shrinking, but for some time I couldn't see anything but the hallucination of colors, swirling around me.

I guess the dragonfly's "visual cortex" (whatever that was) grew in then, because suddenly what I was seeing made sense. At least as much sense as "bug vision" ever makes.

Lots of insects have compound eyes, which means that instead of forming one big, neat picture the way human eyes do, they break the world up into thousands of separate images. It's like looking at a wall of a thousand TV sets, each one tuned to a very slightly different angle. It's a mosaic. You can see it as one big picture, but it takes work to "humanize" the image.

But this wasn't just bug vision. This was Super Bug Vision. This was Mega Bug Vision. It wasn't like facing a wall of TV sets, it was like being inside a dome with tiny TV sets in front, to the sides, above, behind. . . . And I didn't have to turn to see in all those directions. I could see them all simultaneously.

Up, down, left, right, forward, back, all at once.

So I had a really good view as my legs grew

sharp spikes. And I could see quite clearly as the extra set of legs erupted from my chest like hyperactive worms crawling out of an apple.

And I didn't miss any part of the show as my shoulders turned green and bulked up like I was wearing football pads. And I definitely saw the way my butt — yes, sorry, my butt — suddenly began to grow. And grow. And grow. Out and out and out.

I saw backward over my green shoulders as two sets of wings, each translucent and veined like a leaf, grew straight out to each side.

I was shrinking all this time, but I noticed something interesting. When you shrink to housefly, pretty soon you can't make out anything further than a few feet away. But with dragonfly eyes I could still see Cassie quite clearly, towering above me like the World Trade Center. From down on the ground I could see her face! Of course it was mostly purple, and her eyes seemed to glow in an almost radioactive way, but it was still Cassie.

I felt myself stop shrinking. I looked around. Something I could do without looking around at all, if you understand what I'm saying. I seemed to have completed the morph.

I waited patiently for the dragonfly's instincts to kick in. Waited . . . noticed a tiny beetle crawling beneath me. Waited . . . saw the way the fallen leaves looked like starched blankets piled up. . . . Waited . . .

Movement in the air above me!

MOSQUITO!

I don't even remember leaving the ground. It happened too quickly for me to notice. One second my dragonfly vision had spotted something buzzing and fluttering across my millions of tiny TV sets, and the next split second I was in the air.

I was two inches long, going from zero to thirty-five miles an hour in the blink of an eye.

The mosquito never saw me coming. He was helpless. He was a Piper Cub and I was an F-15. He had no moves. He had no speed. He lumbered around in a kind of wandering, meandering nonpattern, and I came in on him like a hungry shark on a kid in an inner tube.

I opened my powerful jaws and hit him going full speed. My bony head smacked the mosquito's body.

My jaws closed on a crumple of legs. The mosquito struggled briefly, legs kicking, wings still trying to fly.

It had all happened in a flash. Less than five seconds passed from liftoff to swallowing half the mosquito.

That's how long it took me to regain control. At which point I realized that there were parts of a mosquito sticking out of my mouth.

And unfortunately, I had a really, really good view of the parts.

CHAPTER 11

<Aaaaaahhhhh! Would you slow down?> Marco yelled.

<I'm not going that fast. Besides, how can you tell how fast I'm going? You're a flea. You can't see squat,> I pointed out.

<I can feel the wind off your wings! It's like a hurricane. If we fall off we'll have to demorph right in the middle of the beach.>

I was still in dragonfly morph. The view back along my body showed my long, blue-green abdomen. And crouching on my abdomen, sitting like creepy passengers in disorderly rows, were five fleas.

<Hey, I want to get there, all right?> I said.

<You think I like having five fleas with their bloodsucking mouthparts stuck into me?>

<*You're* complaining?> Marco shrilled. <We're the ones sitting here while you go zipping around playing *Top Gun.*>

<Aww, shut up, Marco,> Rachel said good-naturedly. <It's kind of fun. The wind whistling through the chinks in my body armor, rustling the spikes on my legs . . .>

<You people are all crazy,> David said.

<At one level, it's kind of fascinating, you know?> Cassie said. <I mean, did anyone ever read the Miss Spider books? *Miss Spider's Tea Party*, *Miss Spider's New Car*? This could be *Miss Spider Goes Flying.*>

<You people are *all* crazy,> David repeated.

<Dragonfly Airlines,> Rachel said with a laugh.

<We cannot go any slower,> Ax pointed out. <It took a long time for all of us to get aboard this insect. Added to the time it took for Tobias to fly us here, we have no more than twenty minutes left in morph.>

He was right. It had sounded easy, getting five fleas onto a dragonfly. It had ended up being a Three Stooges movie. Fleas don't jump all that accurately. It had taken an hour of fleas catapulting like lunatic trapeze artists through the air to get all five of them aboard.

<How are we doing, Tobias?>

Tobias was a few hundred feet overhead, doing everything in his power to look like a hawk minding his own business. Unfortunately, red-tails don't hang out by the water, usually. I needed Tobias to guide us into the resort compound. The dragonfly eyes were very good for a bug, but still not good enough to see the thousand yards that separated us from the Marriott's outer wall. Whereas Tobias could easily keep track of a two-inch-long dragonfly.

<You're wandering a little to your left,> Tobias said. <Straighten up. Yeah. That's good. You're on target and closing in fast.>

<It's like watching tapes from Desert Storm,> Rachel said. <You know, like Tobias is the jet pilot, and we're the "smart" weapon going for the target.>

<You put your wars on television for people to watch?> Ax asked. He sounded shocked. <Humans!>

<Wall coming up,> Tobias reported.

<I see the trees,> I said.

<I don't see a thing,> Marco said. <But I'm bloated on dragonfly juice.>

The trees loomed up, more red than green in my dragonfly world. Huge branches reached out for me. I zipped on through.

<Okay, I'm going higher,> Tobias said. <I

want to get out of range of that bald guy with the killer eyes.>

I saw the main hotel building ahead of me. It was suddenly psychedelic red and orange, but it was definitely the building we were aiming for.

Just one problem.

<Tobias. Can you see any open windows?>

<That's what I've been looking for and no, I can't.>

<We can drop down and go in through the front door,> Rachel suggested.

<The lobby will be full of people,> I said. <We're small, but we're not invisible.>

<I have a crazy idea,> Tobias said. <The bellmen and all? They have these kind of tall hats as part of their uniforms. And they keep tipping their hats to the guests before they pick up their bags.>

<That's very polite of them. Who cares?> Marco asked.

<Well, they raise their hats off their heads . . .>

<Don't even!> Marco protested.

<You want us to zip in under some guy's hat?> David asked. <It would take split-second timing. And then he'd have to not notice this two-inch-long bug on his head.>

<Dragonflies can hover,> Cassie pointed out.

<Let's do it!> Rachel said.

<What is a hat?> Ax asked.

I didn't have any better idea. Neither did anyone else. Believe me, I was very open to hearing another suggestion.

<Okay, let's give this a try,> I said.

I swooped down at top dragonfly speed toward the main door of the hotel. Limousines were stacked up waiting. Security guys were everywhere. Uniformed Marriott employees were trying to squeeze through the security guys to do their jobs.

<Again, I have to ask: What is a hat?>

<A hat is something people wear on their heads,> Rachel explained to Ax. <A type of clothing.>

<Ah, yes, clothing,> Ax said disapprovingly. <Head clothing. Of course. Is there any part of a human that cannot be clothed?>

<Yeah, the face, which is too bad when you consider Marco's face,> Rachel said.

<Hey, you know I'm the cutest flea you've ever seen,> Marco replied. <No one has prettier bloodsucking mouthparts than me.>

I ignored all this and focused on the crowd of people ahead and below me. It was easy enough to make out the scurrying bellmen. And their hats were easy enough to spot. The trick was finding a bellman who was just about to . . .

<Whoa!> Cassie cried.

I had just kicked it into overdrive. I saw the hat. I saw the hand reaching up for the hat. Back of the hat coming up . . . higher . . . higher . . . an opening!

Zoooooom!

Under the brim! Sudden shadow. My eyes couldn't adjust. I couldn't see —

Bumpf!

I ran into a curved wall of felt. It was the inside front of the hat. I fought to keep my altitude. If I landed on the guy's head, he would definitely notice.

And then the lights went out. The brim was back down. I hovered, wings buzzing like mad.

The rear wall of felt raced at me. He was moving. I held onto my hover, trying to stay in the exact same place without moving. Which, by the way, is almost impossible when all you can see is a very dim, blank circle of felt all around you.

<I'm fighting this overpowering urge to jump,> Cassie said. <The flea is smelling the guy's head!>

<Me, too, but we have to maintain,> Rachel said. <No jumping, no biting!>

The trip from the front door up to the guest room only took five minutes. But people who say time is relative are right. That five minutes lasted for hours.

CHAPTER 12

I hovered and I hovered and I hovered some more.

The bellman and the guest were talking.

"So, you work for CBS News, huh?"

"Yep."

"You know Cokie Roberts?"

"She's at ABC."

"Oh, yeah. So, do you know her?"

"Nope. But I know Dan Rather."

"Uh-huh. That Cokie, though, she's hot. I mean, for a news person and all? She's hot."

And at long last, I saw what I was waiting for. A crescent of light! The bellman was tipping his hat again!

I blew out of there at top speed. Out beneath the brim! I headed for altitude.

"Hey, something just flew out of your hat!"

"Whatever you say, sir. You know who else is hot? Bobbie Battista. You know her?"

"She's CNN."

I shot toward the ceiling, cranked a hard right and went skimming at rocket speed. The textured white plane of the ceiling just an inch above me. I spotted curtains and did a neat loop down behind them. I grabbed some curtain rod and hung on, waiting for my stomach to catch up.

<We're in,> I announced.

<Now what do we do, Prince Jake?> Ax asked.

<Wish I knew. We need to get a look around this hotel.>

<Our time is running out,> Ax reminded me.

<We can't demorph with this guy in the room,> Cassie said.

<We have to find an empty room fast,> I said. <I think I know the way.>

I zoomed off, skimming just below the ceiling. My goal was a rectangular grate at the top of a wall. The air-conditioning vent. Was there room enough for me to squeeze through?

I aimed for the vertical opening, turned sideways, folded my wings back and shot through.

<Yee-hah!>

<What yee-hah? What are you yee-hahing about?> Marco asked.

<We're in the air-conditioning vent,> I explained.

<It is chilly,> Cassie remarked.

<We must demorph very soon,> Ax pressed.

I zoomed down an endless square tunnel. There was plenty of light from the various room vents. I zipped along, pausing only to glance into each room we passed. They were all occupied. A lot seemed to be reporters just unpacking. In one I saw what looked like Japanese security guys setting up equipment of some kind. But nowhere we could demorph. It was getting desperate. As Ax kept reminding me.

<Prince Jake, there are only five of your minutes left.>

Then . . .

<What the . . . ?> I stopped flying. I was looking out through the vent at a huge ballroom. But it wasn't the ballroom itself that made me stare.

<What is it?> David demanded. <Can we demorph?>

<No. We definitely cannot demorph here,> I said, staring at the incredible scene through my compound eyes. <We have to get out of here.>

I took off again, searching, searching, room after room.

<I am not getting trapped in flea morph,> Rachel said.

<We have three minutes,> Ax said as calmly as anyone could possibly say those words.

We reached an intersection of ducts. Straight? Left? Right? The vent to the right looked darker. Dark was good. Dark should mean rooms that were still closed up. I turned right.

Instantly I felt something wrong, something off. There was too much dust. Too little air circulation. Too —

<Aaahhh!> Something grabbed me. I was yanked out of midair!

I flapped madly, but I felt myself being wrapped up in tiny, sticky ropes. I could jerk this way and that, but I could not escape. My wings were pinned down. My legs . . .

<What's happening?!> Rachel yelled.

Okay, get a grip, Jake, I ordered myself. I stopped struggling. And that's when I saw.

Radiating out from me in all directions were glistening ropes. The ropes were sticky. Thin but strong. And they formed a pattern. A definite pattern.

<It's a spiderweb,> I said. <We're caught in a web.>

And then, with my all-directional dragonfly eyes, I saw the black, menacing shape hanging in the air above me. Eight legs. Eight cold, evil eyes.

The deadly jaws worked, open, closed, open, closed.

I was trapped in the spiderweb. And the spider was home.

CHAPTER 13

Trapped by a spider!

We were in the most secure building in the world. We were surrounded by the security forces of five nations, plus the Yeerks, and I'd been caught by a spider!

The spider advanced, cautious but not slow. It picked its way carefully across the strands of web. I could clearly see its bulging eyes: a pair much bigger, then two pairs of smaller eyes below. And I could see the cruel mouthparts, specifically designed for tearing apart insect flesh.

<Two minutes, Prince Jake!> Ax said.

<I'm demorphing!> David cried.

<No!> I roared. <You'll be crushed inside this

duct.> I couldn't break loose of the web. At least not without some extra weight.

I began to demorph, maximum speed. I was a two-inch-long insect. A few moments later, I was a four-inch-long insect with some very weird features. The web sagged. I hit the metal floor of the duct.

<What are you doing?> Rachel yelled.

<Aaaahhhh!> Cassie cried suddenly.

<Cassie's hurt!> David yelled.

The spider kept advancing. I kept growing. I was five inches long. Already my dragonfly features were being altered as human DNA began to reassert itself.

My backward vision showed the fleas, separated by more distance now, as the flesh beneath them swelled. But one flea was no longer well.

One flea was oozing blood. Blood was squishing out through the armored plates.

My blood! My morphing body must have created a semihuman artery! The sudden surge of blood pressure had burst Cassie's insides.

My mind was screaming. Cassie hurt! The spider still coming on! My own body this weird mess.

But I was free of the web! I buzzed my wings. Nothing! I was too large. I had to remorph, get back down to dragonfly size.

Shrinking . . . too slow! And now the spider

was bold again, advancing at an eight-legged trot. Its mouthparts were gnashing frantically.

I was morphing as fast as I could. Mostly dragonfly again, and free of the web. But Cassie had fallen off!

<One minute, Prince Jake,> Ax said, with a definite tone of desperation in his thought-speak voice.

<No! I'm not getting trapped like this!> David screamed. <No! NO! NOOO!>

He began to demorph. I buzzed my wings, lifted off, and spun quickly around in midair. I saw Cassie lying helpless on the floor. I swooped down, snatched her up in my jaws, and hauled like I have never hauled before. Back the way we'd come.

But now David was growing, weighing me down!

Too little time!

I saw the grate. I saw the vertical slats. I folded my wings, shot through, and screamed, <DEMORPH! Now! Now! Now!>

Five fleas catapulted off my back and spun through the air, growing larger even as they fell.

<Cassie! Demorph!>

I released her. I watched her tumble away, out of sight as she fell and fell the millions of miles to the floor of the banquet room.

I was shedding the morph by the time I lit on a narrow, curved tabletop.

<I can't get out of morph!> Marco yelled.

My heart stopped beating. <No, no, no! Marco, keep trying! Keep trying!>

I was emerging myself, growing on the tabletop. Wings disappearing, abdomen shrinking, legs thickening.

My own eyes were emerging, and through them I could see someone morphing not a foot away on the table. But it was like no morph I've ever seen. The person wasn't changing, but simply growing.

Growing as a flea. A one-foot-long flea. Larger. Two feet long!

Let me tell you something: There's a reason that insects gross people out. Someday go find a blowup photograph of a flea. And imagine it becoming human-sized.

It stood on six bristling legs. The body was the color of rust. It was narrow, as if it had been run over by a train. It was built of interlocking plates of armor. Its head was a hideous helmet, with a ring of spikes raked back all around the top and sides. At the bottom of the helmet were more spikes, like some horrible parody of a mustache. Two stubby antennae protruded. Saber-toothed tiger "teeth" stuck straight down.

It had two black, button eyes. Dead, soulless eyes.

It was now a flea as large as a dog.

<Marco?!> I cried.

<Oh, please, help me! Help me!>

CHAPTER 14

I could not stand to look at the thing.

<Marco?> I cried again. <MARCO!>

Marco trapped in some hideous, oversized flea body? And Cassie . . . what had happened to Cassie?

Suddenly, over the edge of the table, she appeared. She was fully demorphed. Her own self, even though I was still only halfway through the process.

She looked right at Marco. She placed her hands on his sides, ignoring the sting of his bristles as they poked into her skin.

The flea . . . Marco . . . tried to jump. But the legs that could fire a flea through the air were too weak to move the huge thing he had become.

"Come on, Marco," Cassie said calmly. "Clear your mind of all the fear. You can do this. You will morph. Focus on the picture of yourself. Form the picture in your mind. Let go of the fear and focus on the picture of your own body."

We were all demorphing. Rachel's head rose up above the table edge, then David, Ax. One by one they assumed their own forms. One by one they registered horror on their faces.

We all stared. Stared at the monstrous flea. And at Cassie.

And then, slowly, slowly, the armor plate began to soften into flesh. Slowly the mouthparts retreated. The spiked helmet melted into hair.

Slowly, slowly, Marco emerged.

At last he was sitting, his own self again, on the edge of the table. He looked at Cassie with his own, human eyes, and he did something I didn't think Marco was capable of. He put his arms around Cassie's shoulders and cried.

"Thank you," he whispered. "Thank you, Cassie. You saved my life."

The rest of us were left staring at Cassie with expressions you could only describe as awe.

Rachel moved close to me and whispered in my ear. "Well, that sent a few chills up my spine."

I nodded. "Oh, yeah."

"That was like some kind of miracle," David said.

Marco slid off the table and wiped away his tears with the heel of his hand. Ax sent me one of those hard-to-define Andalite smiles, something they do with their eyes alone. <I do not believe in miracles. I always said Cassie had a talent for morphing. And yet . . . this is something I have not seen before.>

"Okay," Marco said, snapping us all out of our trance. "Anyone bothered to notice where we are?"

I shook myself back to reality. "Yeah. I noticed before when we flew past earlier. That's why I didn't come here. Until we had no other choice. Ax! Stay alert, keep your tail ready. Rachel? We may need some firepower."

"What the — what is all this stuff?" David wondered, looking around the room. "And look at this room! It's like, huge!"

<This, unless I am mistaken,> Ax said calmly, <is a small-scale, portable Yeerk pool.>

We were standing in one corner of the ballroom. It was three times the size of our school cafeteria. There were rows of long tables, covered in white tablecloths. Overhead were massive crystal chandeliers. A red carpet with a floral pattern was all around us. All around, except in a

circle where we were standing. At each corner of the room stood a massive, ornamental marble pillar, maybe ten feet in diameter.

And yet here, in one corner of the room, was a stainless steel tub about half as big as a backyard hot tub. Right where a pillar should have been.

"No way!" Rachel said, even as she began to morph into a grizzly bear. "Someone would have noticed, duh. There are security guys everywhere."

At that point her mouth became a muzzle.

"Rachel's right, there's no way to hide all this here," I agreed. "Unless . . ."

Ax nodded. <Yes, Prince Jake. I believe we are standing inside a hologram.>

CHAPTER 15

"Inside a hologram?" David echoed.

"See the pillars in each corner? There should be a pillar here, right where we're standing. There isn't. Instead there's this mini Yeerk pool. And . . . and that thing."

I pointed at a device that looked like a large, blunt-nosed Dracon beam. It was mounted on the small table where Marco and I had demorphed.

<Interesting,> Ax commented. <It's a holographic emitter. But it's only a relay. Not the basic emitter. Not what is causing this hologram we're in.>

I looked around, trying to make sense of it. We were apparently standing *inside* a massive

marble pillar roughly ten feet in diameter. Behind us there was a raised platform. Not quite a stage, just a platform, with the very familiar podium the President uses. You know — the one with the big, blue presidential seal on the front.

I glanced at Rachel. She was getting very large. Too large for the confined space. "Rachel? Sorry, I changed my mind. Demorph."

<Are you sure? There could still be a fight,> she said, sounding almost hopeful.

I looked up at the ceiling. Between the hanging chandeliers were stained-glass skylights. I could see daylight. I looked back up at the air-conditioning vent we'd come through. The pillar hugged the wall to within three feet on that side, and the air-conditioning duct actually bulged out so that the vent itself was just inches from the "column." The hologram must have been weaker up there, where it was less vital.

"What happens if someone happens to lean on this column or pillar or whatever it is?" David wondered. "They'd have to be using a force field, too, not just a hologram."

Ax nodded in agreement. <Yes. Here is what I believe is happening. The Yeerks precisely targeted a Dracon beam from a cloaked ship overhead. They burned down through the roof and through the column, precisely wiping it out. Then they aimed a holographic emitter of enormous

power down through the hole to replace the pillar they had vaporized. A hologram strengthened by a force field. The force field directs its force outward, of course. We can step out of this hologram at any time. But we would not be able to step back in.>

"So why doesn't the roof fall down?" Marco wondered.

"Maybe the pillars are just for decoration," David suggested. "They probably don't really support the roof. They're just here to look cool."

"So what's the point?" I mused aloud. "The force field is in place. How do the Controllers get in here?"

Ax pointed at a sort of arch made of nothing but thick wire. It formed an invisible door, if you can envision that. <My guess is that this arch blocks the force field. There must be some kind of control device in here. They would simply blank the force field whenever they needed to enter the column.>

Ax shuffled with difficulty through the press of bodies over to a small computer console on the Yeerk pool. He stared at it for a few moments, then pressed a button. Nothing changed.

I stepped out, right through what would have looked like solid marble from the outside. Then I turned and pressed my hand against blank, cold marble. I worked my way sideways to find the

arch. Suddenly my hand disappeared into solid marble.

"It's open," I said. I stepped back through to be sure. "Very weird. The force field may be off, but the hologram is still totally real. You'd swear you're walking through solid marble."

I stepped outside once more. Once again the mini Yeerk pool and all my friends disappeared behind me. I was standing beside a massive, pink marble column.

No one entering the room would suspect for a minute that there was anything different about this column.

"I'm telling you how I want it!" a voice said.

I dove. No questions asked. I dove beneath the nearest table and rolled out of sight. A white tablecloth hung all around me.

I saw three pairs of legs approaching. Two male, one female. I cursed myself bitterly for getting careless. Of course people would be coming and going in the ballroom.

It was weird. I felt alone and cut off. Yet I knew that most of my friends were standing just a few feet away. Inside what appeared to be a marble column.

"I want the main table further back, closer to the podium," one of the men was saying.

"But how do POTUS and the other HOS's get

from the table to the podium?" the woman asked.

I had heard the term "POTUS." It stood for President Of The United States. But what was a HOS? Head of State?

"The President and the other heads of state will rise from their seats and travel down along the table, past the photogs, and around the back of the pillar. Then up onto the podium."

"Tony, that doesn't make sense," the other man said.

Suddenly three chairs were yanked out all around me! Legs were coming at me! Two bare, female legs and four covered in gray, pinstriped suit pants.

The three of them were sitting down.

"Urgh!" I emitted a muffled sound as someone's shoe poked my side.

"Don't tell me what makes sense. I've spent weeks working this all out," the man named Tony said.

"If so, then why did you tell us something totally different this morning?" the woman asked.

"You must have misunderstood what I said this morning," Tony said coolly.

"I don't see how."

"Look, Sheila, let me make this simple for you: I am the White House Chief of Protocol. This

is my show. Who sits where is my business. Your business is to make it happen."

Suddenly, I had a feeling I knew something about Tony the others didn't. I squirmed carefully around, avoiding the various poking feet. I needed to see the bottom of Tony's shoe.

"Tony, you don't have to get —" the other man started to say.

"Look, just do it," Tony said.

"Well, okay, but there will be no time to change your mind again before the banquet," Sheila said, sounding huffy. "You know the Secret Service detail insists on knowing all the specifics well in advance."

"I won't change my mind. POTUS and the others will approach the stage from behind that column. That's final."

They stood up. And at just that moment I saw what I'd known I would: a slash on the bottom of Tony's shoe.

I almost laughed. I waited till the coast was clear and crawled back to the column.

Inside, Ax said, <Prince Jake, I believe we may have a way out of here. The hologram and the force field seem to be weaker higher up the column.>

"That would make sense," I said. "They need it reinforced down low in the strong light, down where people might touch it. That's how I was able to see through the illusion when I passed by in dragonfly morph."

<Yes. I think we could escape by going straight up. Straight through the roof.>

I looked up, out at the sky overhead, and saw a circle of blue that looked awfully inviting.

"Fine. Let's get out of here," I said.

But Ax hesitated. He turned his stalk eyes meaningfully toward the stainless steel tub. <The Yeerks are probably already in place. Do we . . . do we leave them?>

I knew what he was suggesting. It would be easy to finish them off right there and then. But if we did, the Yeerks might simply be able to replace them. And they'd be warned that we knew their plan.

Besides, there was something wrong about killing defenseless slugs. I was pretty sure of that.

I shook my head. "Let's fly."

Some decisions are smart. Some are dumb. Some manage to be a little of both. This was one of those.

CHAPTER 16

<Tobias! Are you able to hear us?> Ax called in thought-speak.

No answer. I wasn't surprised. Tobias was probably too far off to "hear." We were all going back to seagull morph. But if we flew straight up we would probably emerge from the middle of the roof. It would look as if we'd simply popped up out of the roof. The roof that was being watched by a dozen security guys — and probably the bald man.

We needed a distraction.

"The fire alarm," David said. "I did it once at my old school to get out of taking a test."

He pointed at the small red lever on a nearby wall.

"Okay," I said. "Good idea."

"I'll do it," David volunteered.

"Everyone start to morph to seagull. David? You have to throw it and come running straight back."

"No duh."

"Okay. Ready? Go!"

We morphed. David ran. He reached the switch, yanked it down.

BRRRRRRRIIIIIIINNNNNNGGGG!

David came racing back.

Wham! His foot caught on a chair leg and he sprawled, hitting the ground.

A split second later, the door of the ballroom burst open. Four armed men came running in, guns drawn.

In a flash I realized my mistake. Yes, the fire alarm would distract the regular guards. But the Controllers would hear the alarm, too, and come rushing straight here — straight to their concealed Yeerk pool.

David rolled under a table, out of sight.

Instant decision time. "Everyone finish morphing and get out of here! Now! I'll get David."

"But —" Rachel said.

"Not now, Rachel," I said through gritted teeth. "Close the archway behind me. David and I will find another way out." I dropped to my knees and crawled out of the pillar. I was out of

sight of the advancing Controllers as I made my way under the table. But peering down the long line of chair legs, I saw David.

Only David wasn't David anymore.

Cassie had helped him to acquire a combat morph. He'd chosen a male lion. As I watched, I saw the bushy mane sprout from around his neck.

I mouthed the word "no" silently. We needed to escape, not fight. But David just grinned. He was still grinning as three-inch-long yellow canine teeth grew from his suddenly puffy upper lip.

"Bar the door!" one of the Controllers ordered. "Push a couple of tables up against it. I'll use the secure link to contact our people. We can't have any of the other security forces barging in here."

I saw feet moving. I heard a table being shoved across the carpet to block the main door.

"Okay, if we have Andalite penetration, they could be anything. Even flies. It's probably just a false alarm. Nothing to do with us. We'll know as soon as we check the pool. If it was Andalites. . . . Well, our friends in the pool will not be alive."

I breathed a small sigh of relief. We'd left the Yeerks in the pool alone. If I could keep David from doing anything crazy, we'd get out of this okay. The Controllers just had to check the concealed Yeerk pool and see that their brothers were alive.

I began to crawl, with infinite caution, toward David. He was maybe thirty feet away, his face concealed by the gloom and the chair legs, and by the fact that his face was changing rapidly.

I kept shaking my head "no." I kept silently mouthing the word "no." I was trying to will him to understand me. But he kept morphing. A long, bushy-tipped tail now extended out from beneath the table.

Legs walked past, almost stepping on the tail.

"Turn off the hologram," the first voice ordered.

I looked back over my shoulder. The marble pillar was there. Then it was gone. Replaced by the stainless steel tank, the narrow table, and the strange-looking "emitter."

Two sets of legs went to the Yeerk pool. I heard a hinge being moved.

"They're okay!" a new voice yelled.

"Okay," the leader said, sighing in relief. "No way we have Andalite penetration then. They'd never leave our people alive. Clear the doors. I'll notify the others. Hologram on."

The pillar reappeared.

David was now a full-grown lion. He was twitching his tail. But it had twitched back out of sight.

I was no more than ten feet away from him. All he had to do was stay still. All he had to do . . .

Legs passed by. David turned his massive head. I saw his hindquarters bunch up, ready for the attack.

I crawled forward as fast as I could, and, in the split second before he would have leaped, I grabbed his mane with my right hand.

Now, let me pause to explain that just because I turn into animals all the time doesn't mean I've lost any respect for them. You see all these lions on TV, in movies, in commercials or whatever, and they're often tame and kind of sweet. Or you see them lying around with their paws in the air, sleeping in the shade on the savanna.

But you need to realize something. The reason lions have lots of time to sleep is that they are very, very effective killers. They don't need to expend a lot of energy, because as long as there is prey, they'll eat just fine.

I grabbed the lion's mane. About a millisecond later it occurred to me that this was David's first time in lion morph. And he might not have control of it.

Which meant I might not have an arm for much longer.

"David," I hissed in a voiceless whisper. "Don't. Do. Anything."

He stared at me with golden-brown eyes. And slowly, deliberately, he drew back his muzzle to reveal his teeth.

"Okay, let's go," the lead Controller said. "Nothing here."

The doors opened. I saw feet walking away.

I was still holding a handful of mane. My face was inches away from David's mouth. And my mind went immediately to the fact that one of the ways a lion kills is by simply crushing the skull of its prey.

Crushing the skull with its jaws till it pops open like a dropped cantaloupe.

<Had you worried, huh?> David said.

"No. I knew you were cool."

<Just being prepared. You know, in case there was any trouble. I was surprised you didn't go into your tiger morph.>

"Yeah. Well, I didn't see the need."

<Hey. You ever wonder who'd win in a fight between a lion and a tiger?>

That took me by surprise. I hesitated.

<Lion. That's what I think. But it would probably never happen,> David said with a laugh.

<It's just interesting to think about. I better demorph.>

Once he was human again, I said, "I think the best way out of here now is the same way we came in." I crawled out from under the table and stood up. "Just one difference. We don't have time to waste having you leaping around in flea morph trying to land on me."

"So what are we going to do?"

"David, I don't want you to take this the wrong way, but bite me."

"What?"

"Bite me on the back. We'll morph together. Hopefully when your flea mouthparts replace your human teeth, you'll remain latched on."

"Yeah, and hopefully I don't do like Marco and end up a two-foot-tall flea *before* I shrink," he said. "That might hurt you just a bit."

The idea worked. And we zoomed madly through the air-conditioning vents till we happened to spot sunlight. There was an outside vent, after all. It had just been well-camouflaged by stonework.

We zipped outside and Tobias snagged us out of midair. We flew home with me mulling the strangeness of David's question.

Who would win a fight between a lion and a tiger? And why did I suddenly care about the answer?

CHAPTER 17

We now knew the Yeerks' plan. They would wait for the big banquet. The heads of state would walk up to the platform, one by one, to give speeches. One by one they would pass behind the holographic pillar.

There, out of sight of the audience, they would be hauled inside the pillar. They would be grabbed and held, their heads forced into the pool. A Yeerk slug would enter through their ears. Minutes later, they would be Controllers.

Meanwhile, the holographic emitter we'd seen would project an image of the head of state continuing his walk up to the podium. He would seem to reappear on the far side of the pillar, walk up, and calmly deliver his speech.

By the time the speech was over, the real head of state would be ready to emerge. The switch would then be done in reverse.

"Tony, the White House protocol guy, is the man with the slash on his shoe," I told the others as we gathered in the barn. "That was the whole purpose behind grabbing the helicopter. It wasn't the President they were after right then."

"They want a grand slam," David said. "They want all these guys at once. So they snagged the *second* helicopter, the one that always accompanies Marine One to throw off possible terrorists."

"Exactly," I agreed. "They needed the chief of protocol, the guy who would decide how the banquet was laid out. So Visser Three acquired him. Replaced him."

"What about the real guy? The actual chief of protocol?" Cassie asked.

"Probably still alive," Marco offered. "Visser Three has him drugged, takes his clothes and shoes, goes out and does his stuff. Then later the real Tony wakes up and doesn't realize anything has even happened."

<Why not just make Tony a Controller?> Tobias asked.

"I don't know," I admitted.

But Ax spoke up. <The buildings where these heads of state work and live are carefully

guarded? And all of the employees carefully watched?>

"You know it."

<Then there may be a simple reason: Kandrona rays. If the President and the others are made into Controllers, they won't be able to get away from the President's security people long enough to secretly visit a Yeerk pool every three days for their needed Kandrona rays. So we have to assume the plan will be for the President to have a Yeerk pool and Kandrona placed within the White House itself.>

Rachel made a rude, dismissive noise. "How would they keep something like that secret?"

David supplied the answer. "Only the President could order something like that done in the White House. And even then, only if most or all of his Secret Service guys and a lot of his staff were Controllers, too."

"The big goal is to get the President and the others," Marco agreed. "They need to get the President under control and he'll then make it possible for them to install a Kandrona in the White House itself. They need a Kandrona right there. They can't have well-known White House personnel secretly running around to Yeerk pools. So they didn't make this Tony guy a Controller because if the whole scheme fails,

he'll be stuck in Washington without access to a Kandrona."

Cassie shook her head. "Very clever, boys, but as usual you've overlooked a much simpler explanation."

"What simple explanation?" I asked.

"Ego," Cassie said. "You have to look at who we're talking about here. It's Visser Three. It's his biggest scheme ever! If it works, the battle for Earth is won. He'll be the big hero of the whole Yeerk Empire. And if it fails, he'll look like a fool. So what's he going to do? Stay aboard the Blade ship and watch? Uh-uh. Not Visser Three. He wants to be there. He wants to be able to say, 'Look, I did it all. Me, me, me!'"

I nodded. As usual, Cassie had seen what I had missed.

Cassie grinned. "Typical males," she said airily, self-mocking. "All you think about is plot. You always forget it's about personality. It's about character. Visser Three has to be there, see. He's an egomaniac."

Marco, David, Ax, Tobias, and I all looked at one another, feeling a little disgruntled.

"I still like our explanation," David said, speaking for all of us.

"Well, I assume this banquet is tonight," I said, looking at my watch. "And if I'm right, we have very few hours to figure out how to bust up this plan."

"I need to spend some time at home," Rachel said. "You probably do, too, Jake."

"Actually, I'm pretty free for now," I said. "You heard about Saddler, right?"

She hadn't. So I told her about our injured cousin. About my parents going to help out. And about the fact that Saddler was not necessarily going to survive.

Everyone made the right noises of sympathy. So did David. But while his mouth was making the right words, I saw something disturbing in his eyes. Something I couldn't quite put my finger on.

I glanced at him and he looked at me with a face that seemed to be shining with restrained excitement. Like someone who had just figured out how to win the lottery.

And I heard an echo of Cassie's words in my mind: "It's always about character."

CHAPTER 18

I didn't know David. I realized that now. I hadn't really had time to get to know him. It had been one crisis piled on top of the next since we'd first learned about David finding the blue box.

I knew each of the others. Name any situation. I could tell you exactly how Cassie or Marco or Rachel or Tobias or even Ax would react. But David remained unknown. Unpredictable.

He'd been brave, mostly. He'd done what he had to do, mostly. But there had been things . . . the way he'd been in eagle morph and attacked some passing bird for no reason. The way he'd gotten weird in the lion morph. And the thing with breaking into the hotel room.

All totally understandable. Nothing really awful. Not given how his entire life had been ripped apart.

He seemed to get along with Cassie and Rachel and Tobias okay. He mostly ignored Ax, like he was afraid of him. Which was easy to understand. Andalites take some getting used to.

He and Marco obviously did not get along. But that was easy to understand, too. Marco is my best friend in the world. But, like Ax, he can take some getting used to.

We made our plans for the banquet that night. And after we were done, with the sun just going down, I gave Cassie a private "follow me" look. We went outside, leaving the others in the barn.

I led her a little distance away, beyond the range of Tobias's sharp hawk hearing.

"You want to ask me about David," Cassie said.

I think my jaw dropped open. "Okay, how did you know?"

"You've been watching him all afternoon like you're trying to figure him out."

I nodded. "Okay. So what do you think? About him?"

Cassie shrugged and looked back toward the barn. "I don't know. I can't seem to figure him out. He's lost his family, his life, his home. He

doesn't seem upset enough for that, you know? I mean, sometimes he acts upset, but . . . I don't know."

"Well, that's helpful," I said, making a deprecating face. "You're supposed to be the insightful one. I'm just a moron when it comes to figuring people out."

Cassie laughed. Then she put her arm through mine. "Take one worry at a time, fearless leader. We have the mission tonight. We have to save the world. Let's do that, then figure out the new kid."

"What do you think of the plan?"

Cassie rolled her eyes. "Ax says it can be done and Marco says it's insane. I agree with both of them."

The plan was pretty simple and straightforward. But it was ambitious, too. See, we didn't just want to save the heads of state. We wanted to force them to confront the truth: that there were aliens among us and that we were under attack.

If we could do that, the world really would be saved.

Ax had explained the way the hologram of the pillar and its force field were created.

A ship, probably Visser Three's Blade ship, was parked maybe ten thousand feet above the hotel. It was cloaked so it would be invisible to radar and eyesight. It had to hold its station perfectly, never wobbling. It beamed the holographic picture and the force field down through the roof of the banquet hall.

It took enormous, unimaginable amounts of energy.

<Especially with inferior Yeerk technology,> Ax had said snidely. <Andalite technology would do it better, of course.>

"But Erek and the other Chee use holograms constantly," Marco pointed out. "Their visible bodies are holograms."

<Yes. Obviously in that one area, the technology the Chee possess is somewhat superior even to Andalite technology.>

"*Way* superior," Marco had said, deliberately busting Ax and grinning the whole time. "Way, way superior. I mean, just so I have this straight, you're saying the Chee technology would be to Andalite technology like human technology is to . . . oh, say, chimpanzees?"

That brought a laugh from everyone. All except David. David's gaze was somewhere else. He was looking at us, but from far off. Like we were each animals at the zoo. Like he was sizing us up.

Ax got the best of Marco in the end. <Actually, the gap would have to be even wider, since there really isn't all that much of a difference be-

tween human technology and chimpanzee technology.>

"Oooooh, score one for the Ax-man," Rachel said.

The basic plan was simple enough. According to Ax, the beams from the Blade ship were focused to be strongest at ground level. The higher you got, the easier it would be to penetrate the beam and get inside the hologram.

From that point on, you could drop straight down to the hidden Yeerk pool.

Just a few major problems. We would have to instantly take out any Controllers who were stationed within the hologram column. And if any of us stepped outside the hologram, there would be security guys on us before we could blink.

Then we'd have to be ready to snatch the various world leaders as they were pushed toward us and convince them to play along. Despite the fact that most of them didn't speak English.

And oh, by the way, Erek had warned us that one of the men, one of those world leaders, was *already* a Controller. At least one of them.

It would be a very strange game.

CHAPTER 19

<Have I mentioned that this is insane?> Marco said.

<Yeah, I think you may have,> I said.

<Have I mentioned that of all the insane things we've ever done, this is so insane that it makes all previous insanity seem sane?>

<I don't think you've mentioned that more than, oh, nine billion times,> I said.

<Well, as long as we're clear on the fact that this is INSANE. In. Sane.>

<Marco, shut up or I'll squeeze harder,> Rachel said.

Here was the situation. We were all in birds-of-prey morphs. We were flying high. Too high for birds of prey at night with no thermals to lift us

up. We were working at it, I can tell you that. We were flapping like idiots, fighting for every foot of altitude.

And to make things worse, we were carrying things. I was carrying a teardrop-shaped lead weight. It wasn't all that big, maybe four ounces, but try carrying even four ounces when you're a peregrine falcon. Falcons aren't all that big.

Tobias, Cassie, David, and Ax were all carrying similar weights: plumb bobs, fishing weights, and even an awl. We'd found them with some old tools and fishing tackle in Cassie's barn.

Rachel was carrying Marco.

And Marco was a snake.

In fact, he was the cobra David used to own. David's snake had been made safe by the removal of its poison sacs. But since Marco morphed from the DNA, the surgery was irrelevant.

Marco was a fully functional cobra, with venom that could knock a horse down in seconds and kill it in minutes.

Rachel, as the largest of us with her bald eagle morph, drew the task of carrying Marco.

We were high above the beach, following the surf line so we wouldn't get lost. There was no moon. Even if there had been, we'd have never seen it because clouds — big, black, rain-soggy clouds — covered the sky.

It felt like those clouds were right on top of us. Actually, they were. As I flew, I'd pass through wisps of their lower edges.

The surf below was bright enough, though. It was a wavy, silvery line, advancing, retreating, but always pointing the way for us. Just in case we had trouble with the darkness, Cassie had gone into a great horned owl morph. Our birds-of-prey eyes were not nearly as good at night as they were in the day. But Cassie could see the individual sand crabs scuttling around hundreds of feet below us.

Ahead and far below, the lights of the Marriott resort were blazingly bright. It was lit up like a Monday Night Football game.

We passed silently over the line of trees that marked the edge of the compound.

<Oh, wow!> Cassie said suddenly. <It's him! Cool!>

<It's who?> I demanded in alarm.

<The President! He's walking from that cottage over to another cottage. Can't you see him? He's wearing shorts.>

<Hey, let's go see if we can get an autograph,> David suggested, and then broke up laughing at his own joke.

<Ax-man?> Tobias asked. <Are we high enough up to be able to penetrate this force field?>

<I believe so,> Ax said. <Probably. Most likely.>

<Well, that's reassuring.> Marco, of course.

<I will go first,> Ax said. <If I appear to run into an invisible wall and am knocked unconscious and fall toward the ground, you'll know the force field is still too strong at this height.>

Was that Andalite humor? I could never be sure.

Ax pushed a little extra power into his harrier wings and pulled ahead. We watched him fly over the banquet hall, directly over the place where we knew the hologram/force field entered the roof.

He seemed lost for a moment, going this way and that, then . . .

<I am inside!> he said. <Hah! We're only two hundred feet up! An Andalite force field would be ten times this strong at this distance from the focus point.>

He flew in a very tight circle, staying within the beam. We flew to catch up with him. There was an itchy, creepy-crawly sensation as I flew through the perimeter. Like ants covering my feathers. But then I was in. And now, looking down, I could see straight through the perfect circular hole in the roof. It was light down there. Light enough for me to see the heads of three Controllers.

<Three of 'em,> Rachel said. <No problem-o.>

We could see the tiny, stainless steel Yeerk pool. And we could see the human-Controllers lurking beside it.

Three heads.

Three targets.

<Ready?> I asked.

<Let's do it!> Rachel yelled.

<I am ready, Prince Jake.>

<Definitely not,> Marco said glumly.

<Okay, I go first, then David, since we're the fastest in a dive. Then Tobias, Cassie, Ax, and Rachel with Marco, you come last. On the count of three. One . . . two . . .>

I spilled air from my wings, flicked my tail, and headed straight down. I flapped to build up speed and I rocketed down that tube.

The fastest thing in the air is a peregrine falcon in a dive. I broke a hundred miles per hour within seconds and kept building speed. Faster and faster, as my laser-intensity falcon eyes watched the head below me grow larger and larger.

I gripped the lead weight in my talons.

I was a dive-bomber. And I was doing well over a hundred miles per hour when I released my bomb.

Now you know why we were carrying the weights.

CHAPTER 20

Down, down, down like a diving fighter plane!

I released the weight, flared my wings just a hair, slowed, and swept aside as David's own bomb dropped past me. My lead weight dropped. David's dropped. Then, more slowly, three more weights.

Thunk!

Thunk!

The first two Controllers went down like someone had . . . well, like someone had dropped a very fast-moving lead weight on their heads.

I mean, they just dropped. The third guy was gaping at them when a near miss hit his shoulder. He jerked aside, avoiding the next bomb.

But the final bomb caught him square on his head, and he fell over the other two Controllers.

We all inscribed tight circles inside the beam as Rachel went blazing past, trailing Marco from her talons.

She flared and killed her speed at the last minute, then dropped expertly down through the hole.

We followed. One of the Controllers was moving, trying to roll over. Rachel released Marco. He dropped directly onto the moving Controller and sank his fangs into the man's leg. He delivered a very small dose of toxin. Enough, we hoped, to keep the guy down but leave him breathing.

One by one, we landed.

It was bizarre beyond belief. We were invisible to everyone else in the banquet hall, but they were not invisible to us.

The place was jammed. Hundreds of people, men in tuxedos, women in gowns. They were sitting at the long tables, and milling around and talking, and leaning over to whisper to one another, and nibbling appetizers and sipping white wine.

And these weren't just people. These were people of the seriously important, powerful variety.

The main table extended straight out from us. The man closest to us could have reached out

and touched us. Only if he had, he'd have felt what he thought was a cool, marble column.

I noticed that one of the lead weights had bounced out of the hologram. It lay at some woman's feet. Fortunately, no one had seen it come flying out of a seemingly solid pillar.

We were all demorphing rapidly, but I think we were all busy being a little awestruck, too. Three places down along the table was the premier of Russia. Down from him? The French prime minister.

I had to resist a powerful temptation to just step out of the pillar and say, "Hey, look at my man Ax, here! Get a clue! Aliens are real and we're being invaded!"

I *had* to resist because there were an extreme number of guys in dark suits with sinister bulges under their jackets and very, very serious expressions.

If I stepped out of the pillar with Ax, there would be about five hundred bullets from five different nations in our bodies before we could say, "Hello."

The subject of this whole summit meeting was the Middle East. I guess people get jumpy when that's the topic under discussion. And the guys in the dark suits and shoulder holsters were probably jumpy to start with.

We demorphed and stood there, crammed together around the stainless steel Yeerk pool. Ax had to keep his tail held close to keep it from showing. I didn't even want to think about what would happen if that tail blade suddenly appeared from the middle of a marble pillar.

"Now what?" Rachel mouthed silently.

"We wait," I said just as quietly. Although as noisy as the room was, we probably could have yelled and not been heard.

We waited as the President sat down and was greeted with applause. We waited as they served soup. And then we waited as they served a salad. And waited some more as they started serving fish.

Something tingled the back of my neck. Something wrong. Something . . . I nudged Cassie. "Didn't you say you saw the President outside?"

She nodded and gave me a quizzical look.

"You said he was wearing shorts. Now he's in a tuxedo."

She looked confused. "I must have been mistaken," she whispered. "Must have been some guy who looked like the President."

One of the Controllers we'd knocked out started to stir, so Marco morphed back to cobra and gave him a mild dose in the leg.

Then came dessert. And the sad thing was, I was starving. I mean, I could have reached out

and grabbed a dessert off the table, that's how close I was. It was weird. Like being the invisible man.

But at last came the speeches.

"Get ready," I said quietly, rousing the others, some of whom were half asleep from boredom. "Let's get these guys' suits and ties. Um . . . not you, Rachel. Or Cassie. I kind of think this is a job for the boys only."

It took about five minutes, but soon we had three suits of clothing and three unconscious guys in boxers and undershirts.

Ax, David, and I each acquired one of the unconscious Controllers.

I know what you're thinking. We have a rule against morphing other humans. But to my mind, these weren't really other humans. The bodies may have been. But their minds were pure Yeerk.

Besides, there was no other way. Even Cassie had agreed for this one time. If we didn't pull this off, the leaders of the free world would be made into slaves of the Yeerks. That couldn't happen.

Ax began to morph a guy in his late twenties. David and I began to morph into what could almost have been some version of ourselves twenty years from now. Rachel and Cassie turned discreetly away.

It was an easy morph. But to tell you the

truth, it was weird, anyway. There was something just wrong about using someone else's DNA like that. Something . . . creepy. At some level, we were doing something very close to what the Yeerks were doing: We were taking control of a human being.

Not their minds, of course. Because morphing just gives you the body and the instincts, not the memory, the thoughts, the soul of an individual. Basically, we were cloning these three unconscious men. Making exact duplicates of their physical selves.

For me, the actual morph was a big nothing. I looked different, but I didn't feel any different. Just taller, heavier, and like I needed a shave.

I quickly donned the man's suit and slipped the still-knotted tie over my head. As soon as Ax had human arms we slipped his Controller's suit and shirt on him. We'd all seen Ax try to put on "artificial skin," as he called it. We didn't have time to wait around for him to figure out the difference between arm holes and leg holes.

Then we tried to put on the tie. Just one problem: Cassie had picked up the tie he'd dropped and nervously unknotted it.

None of us guys had a clue how to retie it.

For about ten seconds, Marco and David and Tobias and I just stared at one another and at the tie and back at one another.

Then Rachel whispered, "Oh, good grief, you guys are pathetic. None of you has ever tied a tie?" She snatched the tie out of my hands, whipped it around Ax's neck, tied it neatly, cinched it up, rebuttoned his shirt using the buttonholes we'd managed to miss, buttoned the top button of his jacket, straightened his lapels, and pushed his hair into place. All in less time than we'd wasted staring blankly at one another.

She grabbed one of Ax's shoulders and spun him around to face the "doorway" in the force field.

The Yeerks' plan was simple. Wait until one of the presidents or prime ministers disappeared behind the marble column. Then, when the hologram was opened for just a split second, the two Controllers waiting there would shove their victim inside.

The hologram emitter would project an image of that same leader walking to the stage and giving his prepared speech.

When the speech was over, the man would appear to walk back behind the pillar. At which point the real leader, now a Controller, would step out, and boldly sit down with his wife and aides.

Our plan was equally simple. We'd wait till the Controllers outside shoved the President or prime minister our way. Then we'd grab him and let the emitter show the guy heading up onto the stage. Meanwhile, we'd explain to the man what was happening. We'd show him the Yeerks. We'd have Ax demorph to demonstrate that he was, in fact, an alien.

Then we'd let the guy go and repeat the process with each new leader.

Insane, yes. But it was all we could think of. And it could have worked.

Could have. If . . . if I'd stopped to think about just how well a great horned owl can see at night. And just how recognizable the President is. And just how long it takes to put on a tuxedo.

CHAPTER 21

Someone was up on the podium doing an introduction. You know: "Ladies and gentlemen, I present to you a great man, a man of the people, but also a man of history . . ."

Two burly-looking guys in dark suits edged up behind the pillar, on either side of the "door."

The room burst into applause, and one man stood up and headed down the table toward us — toward what he saw as a marble pillar.

"Which one is he?" David whispered.

"The French prime minister," I said. "I think."

The French prime minister walked toward us around the back of the pillar, and . . . walked straight on by, up to the podium.

We looked at one another in confusion.

"He must be the one who is already a Controller," David said.

I nodded. But I wasn't too sure. Something was bothering me. Hovering just out of reach in my brain. I'd had that feeling before. That terrible feeling that I'd missed something.

Unfortunately, like most premonitions, it was useless. Because usually that kind of premonition turned out to be wrong.

Still, I tried to focus, tried to figure out what was nagging at me.

The French prime minister spoke for about ten minutes, then went to sit down. Another introduction followed. And then the Russian premier headed toward the podium.

We tensed up again. He came closer, closer . . .

This time it had to happen. Erek the Chee had always had excellent sources of information. And Erek had said only one head of state was definitely a Controller.

The Russian premier walked past. And on up to the platform. He began talking, pausing every few seconds for the translator to translate his speech into English.

That's when I knew.

"Oh, man," I whispered. "It's a trap."

For a moment, I couldn't do anything. I couldn't think. I couldn't even breathe. I just stood there, reeling.

Then, I realized I knew one thing, at least. "Battle morphs! Now!" I hissed.

No one asked why. No one hesitated.

I demorphed to my own body. Without waiting, I began to grow orange-and-black-striped fur. But before I morphed completely, I grabbed Ax's now-Andalite arm.

"A hologram inside a hologram. Is it possible?"

His eyes went wide in shock, then in anger. He didn't have to answer.

I was halfway to tiger when the Russian premier started laughing. He was standing at the podium just laughing, although he still seemed to be delivering his speech. He was looking out at the audience, speaking Russian. But now, from within the Russian premier, came the sound of laughter.

<Has the truth dawned on you yet?> a familiar thought-speak voice asked. <Do you realize what has happened? Come, come, surely you must know it now. Surely such brilliant fighters as yourselves must have figured it out.>

From the very middle of the Russian premier, a hooved leg emerged. Then a pair of stalk eyes, an arm.

Visser Three stepped out of the Russian. Out of the *hologram* of the Russian.

The Russian kept talking. The audience kept

nodding appreciatively and interrupting with applause. But none of it was real.

We were inside a hologram of a marble pillar. But the hologram of the marble pillar was inside a hologram showing a room full of people.

A hologram showing a president who in reality was outside. Wearing shorts, just as Cassie had seen him.

<Turn off the outer hologram,> Visser Three said.

Instantly the entire room full of people disappeared. All the heads of state. All the guests. All the food. All the sounds of laughter and applause and conversation.

It all disappeared. Instead, we saw the banquet room itself. Empty, except for the rows of tables and chairs.

That, plus a solid wall of Hork-Bajir warriors completely encircling us, each with a Dracon beam leveled directly at us. Or at least at the marble pillar they could see.

<Now,> Visser Three said with exquisite enjoyment, <now, you may turn off the inner hologram.>

We knew that the marble pillar had disappeared. We were now exposed to the army of Hork-Bajir. And not three feet away from Visser Three himself.

We stood there, a strange collection of animals: a tiger, a lion, a bear, a hawk, a wolf, a snake, and an Andalite. We were a formidable force. But we were nothing compared to the small army that surrounded us.

If one of us had so much as twitched, thirty or forty Dracon beams would have fired instantaneously. And a split second later we'd have been nothing but atoms.

<By the way,> Visser Three gloated. <The *real* banquet is tomorrow night.>

CHAPTER 22

Trapped!

We had a simple choice: Surrender or die.

Only in reality, it was worse than that. Even if we surrendered, there was no guarantee we'd live. And at the very least we'd be made into Controllers.

<Let's get them!> Rachel said. <What do we have to lose? At least we can take a few of them down with us!>

<No, we can't,> Marco said flatly. <We'll never even lay a paw on any of them. We won't get two feet before they fry us.>

<Are we going to die?> David wailed.

Cassie nuzzled against him, comforting him — as much as a wolf could comfort a lion.

<Demorph,> Visser Three ordered. <Don't worry, I have no desire to kill you. After all, six Andalite host bodies? It would be a great accomplishment for me. All of my most trusted lieutenants could have morphing power. That, plus making hosts of the most powerful leaders of this planet? I'll be Visser One before the week is out! Hah-hah! I'll be sitting on the Council of Thirteen within a year!>

I swear the evil creep practically danced with glee. The urge to at least take a leap at him and maybe, just maybe, get my claws on him was so powerful I almost couldn't think straight.

But at the same time, something was bothering me about what he'd said. About several things he'd said. Starting with the fact that he'd said there were six of us. He couldn't have overlooked a lion, a bear, a tiger, or a wolf. Certainly he didn't overlook Ax.

I tried to glance sideways and see the others. I could make out Tobias, sitting right out in the open where Visser Three had to see him. Which left . . .

Marco!

You might just overlook a snake. Especially if that snake was behind the stainless steel pool.

<Marco! Can the Visser see you?>

<Probably not, but about nine thousand Hork-Bajir can!>

<Marco . . . are they looking at you? I mean, are any of them looking at *you*?>

<Actually, no.>

I felt like my brain was working in slow motion. Visser Three didn't see Marco. His Hork-Bajir didn't seem to be looking at Marco. And Visser Three was still planning to go after the heads of state. All of which meant . . . what?

<I'm growing impatient,> Visser Three said. <Demorph. Do it now. If you refuse, I'll kill you one by one till you decide to comply.>

He raised a Dracon beam weapon and pointed it. The tip of it traveled from one of us to the other. Tobias . . . Rachel . . . Me . . .

<Who dies first?>

<Wait!> David cried. <Don't shoot me! I'll demorph. I don't care about these — AAAHHHH!>

Cassie clamped her jaws around David's right hind leg. Sweet, gentle Cassie.

HHRRRROOOOOWWWWWWRRRR!

David roared in rage and pain. A roar that made my skin vibrate and made Visser Three jump.

Instinctively David jerked around, reaching for Cassie's head with his own fangs. But Cassie

was too clever for that. David spun around, trailing Cassie like an extra tail, but he could not reach her.

<Stop it! Stop it or I'll shoot now!> Visser Three yelled.

<David!> I yelled. <Get a grip! Stop it!>

The Hork-Bajir just kept watching, Dracon beams raised as the weird fight of lion and wolf continued.

And that's when it began to click. Even as I was yelling at David, the last puzzle piece fell into place. <How the heck did he get all those Hork-Bajir in this place?> I demanded suddenly. <We could barely get a dragonfly in here!>

If I was right . . . *was* I right? Or was I just desperate?

<Rachel! Explain to David that he needs to knock it off!> I snapped.

Rachel was on all fours. She half rose up to a sort of bear crouch. She reached out with her left paw and swung hard. She connected with David's snarling, snapping jaw. David staggered. Cassie released David and jumped back.

<Hah! Andalites fighting among themselves,> Visser Three crowed. <But as entertaining as it is, I order you to stop!>

<She bit me!> David yelled, outraged.

<I'm going to kill *you* first,> Visser Three said to David.

<No! I'll demorph! See? I'm doing it!>

<Shut up, you pathetic, gutless weasel,> Rachel screamed. <You won't have to wait for Visser Three to kill you!>

<They're threatening me!> David cried, running toward Visser Three.

And then I knew for sure. Visser Three turned his Dracon beam on David. He hesitated. But more important, none of the Hork-Bajir even flinched.

<I'm on *your* side!> David yelled.

<Bad choice, David,> I said coldly. <Ax?>

<Yes, my prince.>

<A hologram inside a hologram. That's what we had, right?>

<Yes. The hologram of the marble pillar was inside the hologram of the banquet.>

<Any reason — any technical reason, I mean — why it couldn't be a hologram, inside a hologram, inside a *third* hologram?>

<A third hologram?> Rachel said.

<Yeah. A hologram of a whole army of Hork-Bajir,> I said. <A projection. A fake. I don't think they're really there. I think Visser Three is here, and maybe he's got a couple of human-Controllers with him. But that army of Hork-Bajir around us? I don't think this is a *live* show. I think we're watching videotape.>

<You sure?> Cassie asked.

<Marco? You're out of Visser Three's sight. Start moving toward the Hork-Bajir.>

<Attack them? All on my own? Jake, buddy, you better be right.>

<Yeah. I'd better be.>

CHAPTER 23

<I'm slithering,> Marco said.

I waited. If I was wrong, Marco would die first. But if I was wrong, we'd all be pretty close behind him. All except David, maybe.

David was standing beside Visser Three. He was demorphing. But he was demorphing slowly. It would be impossible to tell that he was human. So far. In a few seconds . . .

No! David was remorphing! He was getting more lionlike again.

<Um, Jake?> Marco said. <I just bit a Hork-Bajir on the leg. He tasted like air. I went right through him. Hologram, but no force field.>

<It is a hologram!> I yelled triumphantly.

<There are no Hork-Bajir! Just us and the Visser.>

<Well, well, well,> Rachel said. <I think I'd better just . . .>

<No,> I said. <I'm faster than you are. I'll get him!>

<But *I'm* closest,> David said suddenly.

David was standing just two feet from Visser Three.

<You want to kill someone, you filthy abomination, destroy me first!> Ax yelled suddenly.

A distraction! Good old Ax.

Visser Three swung his Dracon beam toward Ax, and David struck!

A powerful swipe of his massive forepaw, and suddenly Visser Three's legs buckled. He toppled forward. He landed hard on his face and chest, but he kept his grip on his weapon.

David was on him in a flash.

The "Hork-Bajir" just kept watching. But through the hologram, out of the projected Hork-Bajir, half a dozen human-Controllers leaped, guns drawn.

David lunged at the Visser's throat.

BLAM! BLAM!

I saw one bullet come out the far side of David's shoulder, leaving a red hole the size of a quarter. A pinprick to a lion.

But David pulled back. And Visser Three was already morphing.

<Don't use the human guns, you idiots!> Visser Three yelled. <You want everyone in this complex to hear? Draw your Dracon beams!>

My turn to get into the fight. I leaped for the nearest human-Controller. I hit him as he was fumbling inside his jacket. I knocked him back into and *through* the holographic wall of still-impassive Hork-Bajir.

Suddenly we were outside the illusion. We were in the empty banquet room. I rolled off the human-Controller, got just enough distance, and nailed him across the face with my paw.

He went down and stayed down. It wouldn't kill him. But getting hit by a tiger, even with claws retracted, was roughly like getting popped in the jaw by a cement block.

The remaining guards were struggling to draw Dracon beams. David was all over Visser Three, but Visser Three was getting more powerful by the second. I don't know what hideous alien beast he was morphing, but it was dark and large and had more arms than it should.

I leaped at the next Controller I saw, but Rachel loomed up behind him and tapped him lightly on the head. A light tap from a grizzly was more than enough. The man dropped like a sack of potatoes.

But two more Controllers now had Dracon beams drawn and aimed. Cassie leaped!

Tseeeww!

A Dracon beam fired. Cassie howled and fell short of her target. A burn striped her side, as if someone had placed a red-hot pipe against her. I could smell burned fur. The Controller who'd shot her ran up and pointed his Dracon beam directly at her head.

<NO!> I yelled.

Visser Three had managed to push David away, but large and terrifying as the Visser had become, he suddenly discovered he had an Andalite tail blade pressed against his throat.

<Tell him not to fire!> Ax said. <If he pulls the trigger on that Dracon beam, I remove your head.>

Everything froze. No one moved. The only sound was panting.

<A standoff?!> Visser Three practically screamed. <I won't accept that! I have you! I have you at last. You won't escape me!>

Ax pressed his tail blade against the dark, pockmarked lizard skin of the morphed Visser's throat till black blood began to seep out.

Still, the Visser wasn't ready to give in. He'd gone to a lot of trouble to catch us. He'd taken a big risk. And you don't get to be a Visser of the Yeerk Empire without being determined.

<Which of you is the human?> he asked, his

thought-speak voice suddenly silky and insinuating.

Ax was the one to answer. <Humans?> He forced a laugh. <You are losing your sense of reason, Visser. Humans do not morph.>

<I know you found the blue box,> Visser Three said coolly. <I know a human boy named David found it. And I know you Andalite bandits have gotten to him. You either killed him or made him one of you. And killing him in cold blood wouldn't have suited the hypocritical Andalite sense of morality.>

He was demorphing, returning to his own stolen Andalite body. His stalk eyes were reemerging now, and he turned them to look from one of us to the other.

<One of you is the human child named David. It's to you that I'm speaking, David. David? Your parents are with me. They miss you. They would like to see you again.>

<David, don't say a —> I started to say. But too late.

<You took my parents!> David said. <You turned them into . . . into Yeerks!>

<Yes. But we would not do that to you, David. I give you my word. You would be allowed to live free with your parents.>

<Liar,> Ax sneered. <The word of Visser Three.>

<What other choice do you have?> Visser Three continued, ignoring Ax. <We know what you look like. You'll never be able to go out in the world again, David. Never go to one of your human entertainments. Never —>

<Silence!> Ax said.

<Are you afraid for the young human to hear the truth? You see, David? They can't allow you to learn the truth. The Andalites are a race of liars!>

One of the Controllers touched the earpiece in his ear. "Visser! Humans coming!"

<So, what will it be, David?> the Visser asked. <Come with us now. We'll take you to your parents.>

<Don't waste your time, Visser,> Ax said.

"Visser! Humans coming, fast! U.S. Secret Service. We're monitoring their communications. They are searching for the location of all the noises. They'll reach us in minutes!"

Visser Three hesitated still. I could see the frustration on his face. His main eyes were burning with rage.

<Come over to us, David. Go to your old home. We'll watch for you there. Come over to us! We'll make you powerful! Safe!>

Visser Three began to morph again, this time emerging as Tony, the protocol chief. One of the Controllers was already opening a briefcase with one of Tony's suits inside.

<Turn the inner hologram back on,> Ax directed. <Just wait till we are all inside it.>

We drew apart, two armies observing a truce. The Yeerks backed toward the door as Visser Three continued to morph to human.

We edged within the area that would be concealed by the hologram of the pillar.

Ten minutes later, we were away from the resort. Shaken. Filled with doubts. No closer to our goal of protecting the leaders of the free world.

But alive.

CHAPTER 24

We flew home through darkness. I knew the moods of my friends. I knew who would explode and when. I contacted them, one by one, in private thought-speak.

<Don't say a word, Marco,> I warned.

<About what? About the fact that David was ready to —>

<I don't have time to argue, Marco, just *don't*!>

I never do that. I never hand out orders. I mean, I am supposed to be the leader, but I don't give orders. I just don't feel like I have the right. But this time I had no choice. One wrong word, and we could be in bigger trouble than we were already in.

<You guys know I was just faking the big Yeerk out, right?> David said.

<Yeah, right,> Rachel began.

<Rachel. Shut up!> I snapped so only she could hear me.

<I was!> David yelled. <I was never going to surrender! And you had no right calling me a coward, Rachel! Maybe you're a coward!>

<Rachel! Not. One. WORD,> I said. <You hear me? Not one word.>

Then, one by one, I contacted Tobias, Ax, and Cassie. The message was the same: No one disses David. We all accept his story. We all play along like we believe it.

<I mean, look,> David was saying, <I'm the one who took him down, right? I mean, I *got* the creep. Even though Cassie had been chewing on my leg. Which was totally unnecessary.>

<You did great, David,> I said.

<Yeah. I think you almost finished the guy off,> Marco enthused.

<I was impressed,> Rachel said. Then added privately to me, <The gutless, treacherous little worm. He blows with the wind. He turned on Visser Three when he saw we might win.>

David seemed to relax as we flew. Then he went beyond relaxing. He started bragging.

<Like I was ever scared of that guy? No way. Him and me, we had a score to settle. And I

would have taken him down, only the way it played out I couldn't. You know, because they got Cassie and all.>

<Yeah, thanks for holding back, David,> Cassie said. <I guess you saved my life.>

<No problem,> David said.

It went that way all the trip back to the barn. David boasting, us reassuring. And the truth was, I couldn't be totally sure he wasn't telling the whole truth.

My instincts told me he was lying. That he'd gone over to the Visser, and only turned on him when, as Rachel had said, he saw how the wind was blowing.

But I couldn't be sure. All I knew for sure was one thing: We couldn't act like we were suspicious of David. If he was lying, we'd just end up warning him. If he was telling the truth, we'd destroy any possibility of trust between us.

So we had to shut up and play along. For now.

It was late when we got back to the barn. Rachel had to rush home to avoid getting grounded for all of eternity. Cassie had to invent some story about having come across an injured raccoon who got away. Her parents would accept that. Marco was basically toast, unless he'd gotten lucky and his dad had gone out on a date. (Turned out he had not. Marco was going to be applying fertilizer to the lawn *and* losing TV for a week.)

Ax and Tobias had no problems. Neither did I. I knew Tom was probably still out. And with my parents out of town, I wasn't in danger of getting grounded.

I thought-spoke privately with Tobias and Ax. Then I flew home and demorphed. I rumpled my bed and stuck a couple of pillows under the covers to make it look like I was sleeping. I wolfed down some food, carefully leaving dirty dishes around for when Tom came home. He'd see the dishes and figure I'd raided the refrigerator before going to bed. I even left the TV on, something I do by accident sometimes.

Then I morphed again, and flew back to the barn to wait.

I resumed human form, crouching and shivering in the bed of Cassie's dad's pickup truck.

I didn't see Ax or Tobias, but I knew they were there in the night, somewhere.

Midnight. Nothing.

One o'clock. Nothing.

Maybe I was wrong. I hoped I was wrong. If I wasn't wrong, I didn't know *what* to do.

I'll tell you something, though. You don't want to try and be hopeful at one in the morning. It's nothing but depressing at that hour. Cassie's house was dark. Everyone was asleep.

Two o'clock.

It began to rain lightly. Only there's no such thing as "light" rain where you're hunched down on a bag of peat moss in the back of a pickup, wearing bike shorts and a T-shirt.

I crawled stiffly out of the bed of the truck and climbed into the cab of the truck. Unbelievable! The keys were in the ignition.

I turned them to the "on" position and switched on the radio very low. That at least was an improvement.

Two-thirty.

I was wrong about David. If he stayed in the barn, I was wrong. And he was staying in the barn.

I kept playing the scene over and over in my mind. The moment when he said <Wait! Don't shoot me! I'll demorph. I don't care about these —> And then the fight between him and Cassie.

Was David telling the truth? Was it all just a clever plan to get close to Visser Three? Had Cassie just gotten in the way?

<They're threatening me!> That's what he'd yelled as he ran to the Visser's side. All part of a plan?

I was fighting sleep and losing. My head kept falling forward, then suddenly snapping back as I jerked to consciousness. My eyes were bleary from peering at the barn.

And, in fact, I missed it when it happened.

But Ax didn't.

<This is Aximili,> he said, in as loud a thought-speak as he could manage. <We have an eagle leaving the barn.>

Tobias's thought-speak came from somewhat closer. <I see him. Jake? I hope you hear me. Because we have a traitor.>

CHAPTER 25

Tobias came swooping down to land beside me on the back of the truck.

"Follow him," I said tersely. "But don't let him see you. Ax and I will follow."

Tobias spread his wings and took off. But as he left he said, <This won't be easy, Jake. In the dark, his eyes are as good as mine. We'll both be moving pretty slow.>

"Do your best," I said. I had already begun to morph to peregrine falcon.

David had a head start on Tobias. An even bigger head start on me and Ax. Ax was morphing to bird, too. None of us was a great night flyer, but golden eagles are fast. Faster than red-tails.

I hooked up with Ax in the air over Cassie's

barn. The thought entered my mind that I should get Cassie, regardless of the risk of her parents realizing she was gone. But there was no time. And surely the three of us could handle David.

Ax and I flew hard. We kept calling to Tobias, but he was not within range. I couldn't see him. Or David.

Was he heading toward his old house? Was he going to sell out to the Yeerks? Could he be that dumb?

Once again I was faced with the fact that I didn't really know David. He was still an unknown quantity. What was he doing?

I had no one to follow. No way to know if Tobias was keeping up with David.

<Ax? We're going to head toward David's old house,> I said.

<Yes. That seems sensible,> Ax agreed. <When . . .>

Ax seemed about to say more.

<What is it?>

<If David is joining forces with the Yeerks, what shall we do with him?>

<I don't know,> I said.

We flew hard, flapping all the way. We flew above the darkened homes, above the empty streets, above the abandoned businesses.

Every few minutes I would call out to Tobias. But he didn't answer. And slowly, another possi-

bility began to occur to me: That it wasn't just a case of Tobias being out of range.

Maybe Tobias *couldn't* answer.

<Ax? Keep an eye out for Tobias.>

<I am. I do not see him in the sky anywhere.>

<Not in the sky,> I said. <Keep an eye out for him on the ground.>

<You think David may have attacked Tobias?>

<Ax, I do not know what to think. I just keep hoping this is all some big misunderstanding. How do we fight against a traitor? An Animorph?>

<We are close to David's house,> Ax pointed out.

<Visser Three said they'd be watching for him there. Which means they'll be watching for us, too.> I looked down at the house. It still showed signs of the epic battle that had taken place there. The window of David's old room was a gaping hole — shattered glass, splintered wood, siding peeled off and hanging down.

A truck was parked across the street. A brown UPS truck. I'd never seen a UPS truck parked on the street before.

<I wonder how many Hork-Bajir they have crammed in there?> I said.

<I do not see David. Or Tobias.>

<Me neither. But David could be in the house. I'll have to go in and see.>

<Prince Jake, this is a trap.>

<Yeah. I know. The Yeerks are on the lookout for David. But if he's here, do they *know* he's here yet? Maybe they missed him arriving. Maybe he's inside and hasn't been spotted yet. Or maybe he's undecided. Maybe he just needs to think about all this.>

<That is a highly unacceptable number of maybes.>

<Yep. Sure is. Ax? I need you at your most dangerous. And that's as an Andalite. Land in that backyard two houses down. Demorph. And be ready to jump some fences.>

<I should stay with you!>

<No. I'm going in alone. If David can still be reached, that's the only way.>

I'd like to pretend that I was some fearless hero right then. But that wouldn't be real. Maybe there are guys who don't feel afraid when they're facing death. But I think those guys are called lunatics, not heroes.

I was scared. I knew what was in the UPS van. I didn't know what was in that abandoned, scarred house.

What I did know was that I had no time to morph into something else. Or to come up with clever plans. All I could do was fly in and hope.

CHAPTER 26

I swooped down toward that window. Or the hole that had once been a window.

Down through the cold, lifeless night air.

It was a strange scene inside. The battle we'd fought there had destroyed the walls, annihilated furniture, left the place looking like a house that's being demolished.

But someone had dragged the bed back into place. It faced a television set. The set was on, but the picture was dim and snowy.

A golden eagle stood on the upright bedpost, watching the TV screen.

And that's when I saw the other bird. A crumpled mass of feathers lay atop a wadded-up sheet. Blood had seeped into the material.

<Tobias!> I cried.

There was no answer.

The golden eagle turned its head to look a me. <He was following me,> David said. <Trying to stop me.>

A voice in my head was saying *no*. Over and over again till it was one long siren wail. *No, no, no*!

<Tobias!> I yelled again.

No answer.

I didn't know what to do. The eagle — David — was three times my size. I was alone. I strained my hearing, listening for breathing sounds from Tobias.

<David, you can't do this,> I said as calmly as I could.

<Do what, Jake? Turn myself over to the Yeerks? Of course not. You really think I'm dumb enough to try that? That's not what this is about.>

<Then what *are* you doing?!> I roared, suddenly not so calm. <What are you doing, hurting Tobias?>

<Hurting him? Oh, he's dead, in case you were wondering,> David said. <Definitely dead.>

My mind kind of went numb as he spoke those words. I strained to hear breathing sounds from the clump of mangled feathers. But there were no sounds.

I felt very weak. Helpless. How could this be? How could I have let it happen?

<Why are you doing this?> I pleaded.

<What choice do I have? The Yeerks know me. My parents would turn me in. And you . . . you and the others? Hey, you made it clear the other night when I checked into the Holiday Inn, right? What was it you said? Something like: "If you go around using your powers however you want, we can't have you around. You're a danger to us.">

I recognized the words.

<You think I don't know you were threatening me, Jake?> David said. <I'm not spending the rest of my life taking orders from *you*. You and Marco and Rachel and Cassie? You're like this clique or something. Like, do what we say, or you can't be one of the popular kids. My family used to move around a lot. I was always the new kid in school. I got used to being pushed around by the so-called popular kids. That's all this is. This is like you and Marco and Rachel are the cool kids, and I'm just the new kid, right? So you get to push me around? Rachel gets to call me a coward? Because I want to stay alive? I don't think so.>

<You murdered Tobias because you think this is some stupid school thing?!> I yelled.

<Murder? I don't think so, Jake,> he said with a laugh. <He's a *bird*. You may kill a bird, but it isn't murder. I'd never do that. I wouldn't hurt a human. But hey, an animal? That's a different story.>

He stared hard at me with the laser-focus glare of the golden eagle. And what could I do? He was as fast as me. Bigger than me. If he had outfought Tobias, with all his experience, he would outfight me.

<What choice do I have, Jake?> David asked, almost sadly. <No family. No home. Can't even step out in public as a human. Yeerks after me. The rest of my life I live in Cassie's barn? Do what I'm told? Let Marco hammer me? Let Rachel look down her pretty nose at me? And in the meantime risk getting trapped as a flea or something? Or killed? Maybe you want to be the big hero, Jake, but not me. I have this power now. I'm going to use it.>

<The Yeerks will never stop looking for you,> I said.

<They'll never find me. See, all I have to do is acquire some other human morph, right? I can be human for two hours at a time. I even have a person in mind. And using my powers, I can take anything I want. Anything. I can be a millionaire if I want.>

<If the Yeerks don't get you, we will,> I said.

<Yeah, I know,> David acknowledged. <But already there used to be six of you and now there are just five. Pretty soon, Jake, it'll be four.>

That's when the eagle spread his wings, flapped hard, and shot toward me.

CHAPTER 27

The golden eagle was huge! The wings seemed to fill the room. The talons, raked forward and opened wide, would rip me open in a flash.

I dropped backward, flat onto my back on the floor. Something no falcon would ever do. Something David's eagle instincts would never expect.

The eagle flew over me. I scuttled under the bed, my talons scrabbling wildly on the exposed wood flooring. Again, something no falcon would do.

<How long do you think you can hide under there?> David mocked. But I could hear frustration in his voice.

He stuck his big eagle's head down and

peered, almost comically, beneath the bed. He could come in after me, but he'd be crammed in tighter than I was. He'd be unable to move.

He flapped over to the window opening. And when I peered after him, I saw his talons growing. He was demorphing.

A mistake. David might have all my morphing power, but he didn't have my experience. He would be helpless while he was in midmorph. I could escape.

Only I didn't want to escape. Not with Tobias lying dead on the bed above me.

I'd gone into lots of battles against Hork-Bajir, Taxxons, Visser Three himself. I'd always gone in hoping to win. But I'd never gone in consciously hoping to kill.

This was different. I didn't want to escape. I wanted to destroy David. I wanted revenge.

Human feet began to emerge from the talons. I timed it carefully, then I scrabbled back out from beneath the far side of the bed and flapped my wings.

David stood there, maybe three feet tall, still covered in feathers. His face was an eagle's face. But there were human fingers beginning to emerge from the wing tips.

He reached over and clumsily grasped a jagged piece of wood about as long as a baseball bat.

<Come on, little birdie,> he said. <Try for the window, go ahead.>

I flapped hard, making a lot of noise with my wings. But I didn't fly. I skimmed across the floor on my talons, using my wings to get up speed.

David saw what I was doing and tried to bend over to slam the stick down. Just one problem: He was still more bird than human. And birds don't have a waist.

WHAP! The stick missed me, and I was under his guard. Under his guard and now flying straight up, up at his face.

He staggered back. He batted at his face with his half-formed hands. But I was too close and he was too clumsy.

I raked his face with both talons.

"Aaaaahhhhh!" he cried with a mouth more human than bird.

I dug one talon into his emerging nose and —

THUMP THUMP THUMP THUMP.

Footsteps racing.

WHAM! The broken door blew back on its hinges. Hork-Bajir poured into the room.

David was still blinded by my feathers and the blood in his face. I immediately let him go, dropped straight down, and turned for the window. I blew through it with Hork-Bajir claws tearing at my tail feathers.

David leaped! Out the window. I was airborne,

but his falling body slammed me out of the air. We went down together. Hard. The swimming pool was behind us.

David was on his back, but already remorphing.

Hork-Bajir leaped fearlessly out into the dark yard. They were a species raised in the trees. A ten-foot drop meant nothing to them.

FWUMP!

FWUMP!

FWUMP!

Three big Hork-Bajir landed on the grass. Their T-rex feet dug deep into the sod. Their blades flashed dully in the dim light. I lay stunned, my feathers muddy and stiff. David was morphing as fast as he could. His human features were already almost gone.

But neither of us was going to get airborne fast enough to clear the fence and get away. I'd need a running start to get that high that fast, and with the pool behind me I was trapped. The Hork-Bajir ran straight for us.

It would be over in a few seconds. I tensed up, waiting for the blade slash that would cut me in two.

But then, something flew overhead! Over the fence. Over the pool! No, it didn't fly, it *soared*!

Ax cleared the fence and the pool and dropped almost daintily down between me and the advancing Hork-Bajir.

<I thought you might wish some assistance, Prince Jake,> Ax said calmly.

"Andalite!" the biggest Hork-Bajir spat.

<Yes, *Andalite*,> Ax said with all the natural arrogance of his people. <What a pity for you, Yeerk.>

Now, one Andalite is not a match for three Hork-Bajir. But the Yeerks have a very healthy respect for Andalite tails. So the Hork-Bajir hesitated.

They didn't hesitate for long, but it was long enough. Ax reached down, scooped me up in his many-fingered hands, and leaped *backward* over the pool.

<Whoa! I didn't know you could do that!> I said.

<I didn't, either,> Ax said.

Hork-Bajir raced around the pool, coming for us. Now that they were past their first hesitancy, they were fixated on the one Andalite they could see and be sure of.

They abandoned David.

Ax turned around and leaped the fence, facing forward. The Hork-Bajir didn't bother to leap. They came barreling straight through, wiping out the fence in an explosion of splinters and a barrage of noise.

Lights snapped on in neighboring houses.

But too late for the Hork-Bajir. Too late for

them to see that the neighbor on this side also had a pool.

Ax skipped clear of this swimming pool. The Hork-Bajir plowed in.

PAH-LOOOSH!

The three seven-foot creatures weren't going to drown. The pool was only six feet deep. But they weren't going to catch us, either.

Overhead I saw the eagle fly.

<I have to go after him!> I said.

<Wait till I can morph and come with you!> Ax said.

<No. We can't lose him!> I said. <Don't follow me. Get help. Get Rachel, she lives close. She can use her owl morph to find us. Maybe.>

<Good hunting, Prince Jake.>

Normally I would have said "Don't call me prince." It's a running joke between me and Ax. But this wasn't a night for jokes.

<Ax? I think Tobias is dead,> I said. <I think David killed him.>

<That would be a most terrible thing,> Ax said.

<Yeah. Get Rachel. If David's killed Tobias, we may have to do a terrible thing, too. Get Rachel.>

I took to the air and raced after the golden eagle.

CHAPTER 28

He saw me. He knew he was stronger than me in the air, but still he flew on.

On through the night, as fast as we both could fly. We passed over the school. We passed over the construction site where the others and I had first encountered Elfangor and become what we were today.

I thought he was flying back toward Cassie's barn. But he kept going, apparently without any specific idea of where to go.

<You've been a long time in that morph, Jake,> he called to me. <Better demorph.>

<Not as long as you've been in your morph, David.>

<I guess you're right. I was looking for the

right place to do this. But I guess I'll have to take whatever comes up,> he said.

I didn't know what he meant. But then I saw him gliding downward. Down toward the empty mall below us.

He disappeared behind a stack of air-conditioning equipment on the vast mall roof.

I looked back, trying to see if Ax had decided to follow me. But no, he'd have done what I asked. He'd have gone to get Rachel.

Nothing. The sky was empty.

I glided down toward the mall roof, avoiding the area where I'd seen David land.

I came to rest on the gravelly roof, exhausted from the endless flapping. I looked carefully, fearfully into the darkness. I strained my hearing. But no one was near.

I watched to see if David would fly away again. But in my heart I knew he would not. David had picked this place. David wasn't going to run.

I demorphed and soon stood there, feeling out of place, conspicuous. And yet I was invisible to anyone on the ground. A raised edge went all around the mall roof. Behind me and to the right were the walls that rose up to the third floors of the big department stores. I was two floors up above the main mall itself.

I began to morph again.

"All right, David," I said to the darkness. "You want this fight? You can have this fight."

The orange-and-black fur swept across my body.

The long tail extended out behind me.

I fell forward onto footpads the size of frying pans. I tested my claws, extending them slowly from their sheaths.

I felt the tiger's instincts welling up beneath my own. I had done this morph many times. I had long since learned to control the tiger's bloodthirsty instincts.

But I didn't want to control them. Not this time. Not with Tobias lying dead.

I sniffed the breeze and smelled him. I listened and heard the stealthy pad of feet on the gravel and tar paper.

I looked, with eyes that were indifferent to darkness.

He was fifty feet away. His mane ruffled in the breeze. His tail swooshed restlessly back and forth.

<You never answered me, Jake,> he said. <Lion versus tiger. Who *do* you think will win?>

<Let's find out,> I said.

Instantly he was a tan blur, racing straight at me, low to the ground.

So fast! Faster than a human could react. So fast that human prey would not have had time to scream.

But I wasn't human.

Like a runaway train he came at me, yellow fangs bared. I sat back on my haunches, gathering power into my legs and lowering my own sleek head.

We hit! His jaws raked past my ear. I twisted and sank my teeth into his . . .

Into his mane! My teeth closed on nothing but hair!

<Aaaarrrggghhh!> I cried. I felt as if someone had shoved red-hot spikes into my shoulder.

His teeth sank deep into muscle and sinew. I twisted, but that only made the pain worse.

I rolled onto my back. My belly was exposed!

He released my shoulder and darted in for the kill, hoping to disembowel me. But I was ready. I curled my back legs up and slashed!

His head snapped back. Blood flew from his muzzle.

Like lightning, I was up on my feet. Fast as only a cat is fast. With liquid speed and vicious grace.

I was up! But the lion, too, is cat.

The paw hit the side of my head so hard my eyes exploded in fireworks. I jumped away and barely avoided those deadly yellow fangs.

Suddenly we were both circling, circling, head-to-head, tails twitching, waiting for the other to make a careless move.

He was as fast as I was. I was bigger and heavier, but not by enough to matter much. And he had that mane that kept my teeth from the one target they wanted most: the arteries that pumped blood through his neck.

I stared into his eyes. He stared into mine. We were electric! Tingling, bristling, buzzing with power and speed and energy.

He leaped!

We hit, shoulder-to-shoulder, and rolled across the roof.

I was on my feet in a flash. But suddenly I realized I wasn't on gravel. My feet were slipping. My claws had nothing to grip.

I was standing on glass. The skylight!

Below me I saw the dim night-lights of the mall. I caught a strange, unreal glimpse of the Waldenbooks and the Baby Gap beside it.

It was a twenty-foot drop to the upper mall concourse.

David leaped. I couldn't grip well enough to move. So I stood, defenseless, as the tan blur came at me like a truck.

He hit! His mouth was aimed at my throat. I jerked aside, he slammed into me, and there was a huge, world-filling shattering of glass.

Down we fell!

Down we fell, slashing and biting and trying to kill, even as the floor rushed up to slam us.

And then, in midair, twisting to get my feet beneath me, I felt the teeth.

I felt them sink into my neck.

I felt the blood gushing.

The tiger's blood.

My blood.

Falling . . .

Falling . . . and already the darkness . . . the darkness . . .

To be continued . . .

Don't miss

#22 The Solution

The sun was just thinking about coming up as we approached Marco's house. It was already bright as day to me, of course. But I could tell the difference just the same. The black sky was becoming gray in the east.

I felt like I was boiling inside. Like pressure just kept building up in me. Like I was going to explode.

Too much swirling through my brain. Tobias, dead. Maybe Jake as well. David, a traitor with all the powers of an Animorph.

And at the same time, we had the biggest mission of our lives. The heads of state were still meeting. Controllers, including Visser Three himself, were still conspiring to enslave the most powerful of all humans.

It was too much. Way too much. I couldn't think about all that.

One thing at a time, Rachel, I silently told

myself. Priorities: David was number one. Everything else was number two.

David had to be stopped. Before he could stop us.

But still, somewhere in the back of my mind, it bothered me that Jake had sent Ax to get me. Me, specifically. Once he knew that extreme measures might be taken, he said, "Get Rachel."

What did that mean? Was that how Jake thought of me? As some crazed, violent nut who would do anything?

No, of course not. He just knew I was good in a fight. That's all. It didn't mean anything.

Besides, wasn't it true? another part of my mind argued. *Wasn't it true? Wasn't I just the person to call if you needed to kill an Animorph?*

Marco's house. Marco's window. Open.

Open? Did Marco leave his window open? Yes, if he'd already flown out of it. Maybe that was it. Maybe Marco wasn't home, had already left. Maybe he'd sensed we needed him.

But as I wheeled to traverse the back of his house, bringing myself closer to the window, I saw Marco inside, in bed.

<This smells bad,> I said to Ax.

<You have a sense of smell in that morph?>

<I meant it, you know, figuratively. Visser Three laid one trap for us. David laid another. I am finished walking into traps.>

<Agreed.>

<Marco!> I called in thought-speak. <Marco! Wake up! Wake up, now!>

I wanted to see him wake up and look around. I wanted to make sure he was alone in the room. He was asleep face down. He rolled halfway over and gave the blankets a kick.

<Wake up!> I yelled.

Suddenly he sat up and looked around. He scratched his face. Then he looked around again.

<Marco, it's me, Rachel. I'm outside. Are you alone in your room?> He didn't smile or leer. He just nodded. Yes, he was alone.

<Okay, let's go,> I said.

Ax was ahead of me. He swooped down toward the window. Marco stood watching, smiling almost. His hands were behind his back.

Swooooosh! Ax swooped through the window and —

Marco pulled his hands out from behind his back. The Louisville Slugger swung in a short, sharp arc.

WHAM!

The bat hit Ax square in the face. I saw a piece of shattered beak go flying, twirling away like shrapnel from an explosion.

Ax fell to the grass outside. Marco laughed quietly. I saw his sides shake.

But of course, it was not Marco at all.

David. David had morphed Marco.

Ax lay on the grass, unmoving. Marco/David held up one finger. Then another. Then another. One, two, three.

He was counting how many of us he'd killed.

One, two, three: Tobias, Jake, Ax.

But . . . it should have been four! What about Marco?

Of course! Marco was still alive because Marco had been human. David had said it himself: He would never take down a human life. He would only kill animals. A hawk, a tiger, a harrier. Not a human.

As I watched, I saw Marco/David begin to blur. The nose and eyes became subtly different. Now he was just David. But he was still morphing when he stepped back out of sight.

I had to think. David was wiping us out, one by one. What was his next move? What was his next morph? Jake would know. Jake was the leader, not me.

I had to get to Ax. No! That's what David wanted.

No, I had to get to Marco. The real Marco, who was probably unconscious inside the house.

No, wait, that wasn't right, either.

And then the golden eagle came flapping out of the window. Another of David's morphs.

It was one on one. Him and me. Golden eagle

against owl. He was faster. Stronger. But it was still mostly dark and the air was cool, with none of the warm lift it would have later in the day after the sun came up and baked the ground.

He was faster and stronger, but the night belonged to me.

I turned and raced away. He followed. Ax lay still on the damp grass. But he was breathing. And to my infinite relief, he was no longer entirely a harrier.

<Follow me, David,> I said. <We'll see who wins this aerial dogfight.>

<Brave words,> he sneered. <But you're mine. Just like that Bird-boy of yours was mine.>

And that's when the pressure inside me evaporated. I was cold again. Cold as a frozen lake. I knew what to do. And I wanted to do it.

I shouldn't resent Jake for thinking of me, I realized. It's what made him a good leader: He knew all us all. He knew me.

<For you, Tobias,> I whispered. And I led David toward his doom.

<Know the Secret>

ANIMORPHS®

K. A. Applegate

- ❑ BBP62977-8 #1: The Invasion....$4.99
- ❑ BBP62978-6 #2: The Visitor....$4.99
- ❑ BBP62979-4 #3: The Encounter....$4.99
- ❑ BBP62980-8 #4: The Message....$4.99
- ❑ BBP62981-6 #5: The Predator....$4.99
- ❑ BBP62982-4 #6: The Capture....$4.99
- ❑ BBP99726-2 #7: The Stranger....$4.99
- ❑ BBP99728-9 #8: The Alien....$4.99
- ❑ BBP99729-7 #9: The Secret....$4.99
- ❑ BBP99730-0 #10: The Android....$4.99
- ❑ BBP99732-7 #11: The Forgotten....$4.99
- ❑ BBP99734-3 #12: The Reaction....$4.99
- ❑ BBP49418-X #13: The Change....$4.99
- ❑ BBP49423-6 #14: The Unknown....$4.99
- ❑ BBP49423-6 #15: The Escape....$4.99
- ❑ BBP49430-9 #16: The Warning....$4.99
- ❑ BBP49436-8 #17: The Underground....$4.99
- ❑ BBP49441-4 #18: The Decision....$4.99
- ❑ BBP49451-1 #19: The Departure....$4.99
- ❑ BBP49637-9 #20: The Discovery....$4.99
- ❑ BBP76254-0 #21: The Threat....$4.99
- ❑ BBP76255-9 #22: The Solution....$4.99
- ❑ BBP76256-7 #23: The Pretender....$4.99
- ❑ BBP68183-4 Animorphs 1999 Wall Calendar....$12.95
- ❑ BBP49424-4 <Megamorphs #1>: The Andalite's Gift....$4.99
- ❑ BBP10971-5 The Andalite Chronicles....$4.99
- ❑ BBP95615-9 <Megamorphs #2>: In the Time of Dinosaurs....$4.99

Available wherever you buy books, or use this order form.

Scholastic Inc., P.O. Box 7502, Jefferson City, MO 65102

Please send me the books I have checked above. I am enclosing $__________ (please add $2.00 to cover shipping and handling). Send check or money order—no cash or C.O.D.s please.

Name________________________________ Birthdate______________

Address____

City__________________________ State/Zip________________

Please allow four to six weeks for delivery. Offer good in U.S.A. only. Sorry, mail orders are not available to residents of Canada. Prices subject to change.

ANI498

http://www.scholastic.com/animorphs